From the Darkness
Oswaldo Salazar

Translated by Gavin O'Toole

From the Darkness
Oswaldo Salazar

Translated from Spanish by Gavin O'Toole

First published in 2007 by Aflame Books
2 The Green
Laverstock
Wiltshire
SP1 1QS
United Kingdom
email: info@aflamebooks.com

© 2004, José Oswaldo Salazar de León/Universidad Francisco Marroquín

Translation copyright © Gavin O'Toole 2007

First published in Spanish in 2004 as *Por el lado oscuro*. This translation is published by arrangement with the Universidad Francisco Marroquín/Fondo de Cultura Económica de Guatemala S.A.

This novel is based on events that occurred in Guatemala between 1939 and 1941 and the author has included some explanatory notes to elaborate on certain themes. These are marked with numbers in the text and included as endnotes.

ISBN: 0-9552339-4-1
ISBN-13: 978-0-9552339-4-4

Cover design by Ludwig Wagner, www.zuluspice.com

Printed by Guangzhou Hengyuan Printing Co, China

From the Darkness

I am not a woman; I am a novel

Eça de Queirós
Ramalho Ortigão

From the Darkness

I

The lake was quiet, as dark as a bottomless mirror, and the dawn air blew delicately over the water towards the south. Far away to the east the Santa Catarina mountains could be made out, outlined in their hesitant silence against a clear sky full of distant stars, and the nearest black crags stood out threateningly like enormous shadows hurled down upon the soft, ancient curves of Lake Amatitlán.

Nothing seemed to move except the old launches nodding in tranquil slumber along the beach, aground in front of a park planted with acacias smelling of night and jacarandas now blossoming with the last colours of an early Lent. Only the caress of the water on the stones and the dense sand could be heard, the murmur of the small, timid, oblique waves that came and went with the rhythm of calm breath, and the piercing, repetitive voice of the crickets, sending their staccato messages like clocks in the night.

To the left shone the dim bulbs of recently installed public street lighting, one penumbra for each block of the small houses cramped in the square between the Puente de la Gloria and the San Juan de Dios Hospital, from east to west, and between the ascent to the Filón and the mountain's folds, from north to south.

Amatitlán was a town of small adobe houses inhabited by peasants and old land-owning families. Just 25 kilometres from the capital, it was famous at the end of the Thirties as the nearest place of rest and relaxation for the well-to-do. The president himself,

Oswaldo Salazar

'The Man' as they called him, was wont to go there, often at the helm of a fleet of motorbikes, and to organise lunches there with friends and sympathisers of his nationalist cause. He ventured to try different routes, the sinuous trails descending Santa Catarina Pinula, or the narrow old road that went without any detours straight to the lake. He liked to go and supervise, in person, the improvements that he was introducing through his municipal managers, as well as maintenance work on the 'filling', a mound of earth of uncommon dimensions upon which, since the era of Don Justo Rufino Barrios, the railway had passed, its din muffled in smoke, bringing progress and the cut and thrust of modern times.

In other circles, Amatitlán was also famous for its bars, dotted at random around the edges of the town and patronised by mixed-race *ladino* youths with bronzed bodies, mainly from nearby towns and other Central American countries. At weekends and on holidays these were transformed, little by little, into islets of light and bustle as night drew on and until dawn arrived.

That daybreak on the 15th of March 1939 the streets were still empty, the windows dark and tightly shut. One after another, the closed, panelled doors stood to attention as if the residents, beneath tiled roofs damp from the morning dew, were awaiting in silence the terrible arrival of the angel of death swooping through their streets, sword in hand and certain to enter wherever the smallest crack, the slightest carelessness, would permit. The damp air of the Bocacosta foothills blew between the mountains and passed desolately through these streets, from time to time taking its whistle of authority to all four corners of the town. It was the discreet start to an ordinary working day. In less than an hour, candles would start to illuminate the windows and the sun would return once again to disperse the mist over the lake, over the maize plantations. The women would come out after drawing back the bolts and a few minutes later the men would fill the streets, carrying their bags of food and tools on their way to the farms and workshops; some would emerge to wait for the wagons that supplied their vegetable and grain stalls; and, finally, the children would let go of their mothers' hands in order to arrive at school early.

From the Darkness

The previous night, Rogelia Hernández had gone to bed late, worried, and had not been able to shut her eyes for a minute. It was now four in the morning and in the darkness she could hear even the slightest rustle. Lying on her side, she sensed the slow breathing of her brother Félix, who was sleeping, oblivious to everything. Behind them, close to his bed, the air moved the dirty curtain covering the threshold to their parents' room, a space that filled her with terror when she recalled the figure of her father, enraged, shouting and uttering incomprehensible things, and her mother pleading with him in a muffled voice, between sobs, no, please, do what you want to me, but leave them alone. But now silence reigned and the imminence of daily life was the perfect setting for the anguish that Rogelia could not help but feel as she reconstructed, over and over again, the scene in the living room a few hours earlier when, under the expectant gaze of her mother, Pedro, her betrothed, had said come, I want to tell you something, and had become very serious before speaking those terrible words that she had listened to without being able to react and that she had ended up accepting, without knowing how or why.

Soon, in the adjoining room, she heard her parents' beds creak. She had heard them all night, between long intervals of silence, but now she knew that this was different and was the beginning of everything. Rogelia did not move, she waited to hear the rustle of the sheets, her mother's feet seeking her shoes on the earth floor and her first steps, and to see the shadow of her mother's body crossing the room where she slept and heading for the smoky kitchen where, together every morning, they prepared food for the working day.

But this was not just another day, it began earlier than usual and Rogelia knew, feared greatly, the reason for this early start. It paralysed her as she listened to the stealthy moves of her mother, who assumed everyone was asleep. After a few minutes, when she judged that her mother had had enough time to do what she had said she would, Rogelia decided to get up. She heard deep breathing in the other room and assumed that her father had woken. It would be approximately twenty past four. Like every morning, she dressed hurriedly because she hated her brother Félix or her father to see her naked. Ten minutes later she was already helping her mother serve the breakfast of coffee and beans. It was a strange moment. She said good morning to her mother but did not dare mention what she had spoken of the previous night and confined herself to giving a hand and to the silence that the situation demanded.

Carried along by the daily routine, Félix arrived first, and Bartolo, the father, next, and they sat down to eat by the light of a thick candle burning in the middle of the table while Bartolo told the boy about the pasture where it fell to them to work that day and the route they would take in order to get there on time without having to rush.[1] Bartolo was a large man, an experienced old wolf who had worked for and knew all the bosses and foremen in the region, who spoke little but, when he did, took his time to say the things that he knew well, that he had learned over years and that were reflected in each crease of his skin, in the dead passionless gaze that distanced him so much from his family.

Having carried out the first chore of the day, Rogelia sat down to eat with them; but this morning her mother, Mauricia, who usually did the same, went into her room unnoticed by the men until they heard her calling Félix. He got up to see what his mother wanted. Rogelia knew the whole story and would not, for anything, have missed her brother's face when he found out. Several minutes passed. Their father, meanwhile, took the opportunity to ask her why Pedro had left so late and she, hating the way he had of talking to her without looking her in the eye, said no reason, only that the time had flown, and he retorted, slurping the last gulps of his coffee, that she shouldn't let it happen, remember what the neighbours are like, I don't want them going and talking nonsense. And he put the coffee cup on the table like a judge who had just let his gavel drop as the final act of passing sentence.

At this point Félix appeared in the doorway. Rogelia's heart missed a beat when she saw him. He was lost in thought, walking like a corpse oblivious to where he was going. Then he looked straight at her as if to ask if it was possible that she, too, knew what he knew, and she returned his look without speaking, telling him

From the Darkness

that, yes, they were not dreaming, it was true and moreover he should not say anything, just do as he had been told by his mother, who now arrived in a hurry to give them their food while telling Bartolo that she would come to the pasture later because she needed to cut some tomatoes for dinner. Félix finally came to his senses when his father, now leaving the kitchen, pointed to the gourd full of water next to the hearth, and the youth circled around the table to reach it. It was cold to the touch and he knew his father had filled it from the earthen jar as he did every day. He threw it across his shoulder, feeling as if it was the first time in his life he had ever done so. Bartolo was already on his way out, standing in the doorway waiting for him. Without saying goodbye, as if fleeing, Félix crossed the patio and felt for the first time the fresh air of a morning that was still night, not yet light. He saw his father on the threshold, one foot inside and one outside the house, impatient, and felt something he had never felt before – that when all was said and done he was nothing more than a poor, defenceless man, lonely, alien to him and the women now awaiting what was about to happen.

Now he had to follow him, walking in his footsteps in silence towards the south, through the still-dark streets of the town and along tracks that he knew by heart because he had travelled them a thousand times, as it had begun to grow light, skirting the maize fields that had been given the names and surnames of their owners. Félix could just see the feet that guided him in the darkness and, as he followed them blindly, he remembered how happy he had felt the first time he had accompanied his father into the fields, on his back the same gourd that he was carrying now. Just the day before that first trip, his father had told him he would not be going to school any more, enough of wasting time, he was a little man now and could help him in the fields. It had been three years ago when he finished primary school, and since then his enthusiasm had not waned. He did not see himself doing things like studying or entering a workshop or going to the capital to survive thanks to some daily miracle. No. He felt fine about following in the steps of this detached man, full of silences, learning day by day all the tasks his father knew –

weeding, harvesting, fencing in paddocks, cutting coffee, digging furrows with a hoe or driving a team of tired oxen, things that were learned without feeling, without words, only by watching, helping, trying them out when he was by himself or going off to do them alone when his father was sick or had taken other work so that they could earn double. No-one, not even he himself, knew how, at what point, he had learned to do so many handy tasks, and the bosses and foremen now counted on him to do the jobs of a grown man.

Félix continued to tread in the footsteps of his father, footsteps that became ever more visible as they approached the edge of the town and started along the forest trails of lost paths, dead ends and tracks with no return. Daybreak always arrived just as they began to lose their way and started to walk between large mounds of earth and clouds of dust beside the field of maize that, depending on the season, was either shorter or taller than they were. After that, they penetrated the damp shade of the forest of coffee adjoining the pastures where Don Emilio Barrera's milking herd grazed calmly and where, with his permission, they now had to slash the wild undergrowth down very low in order to be able to plant, as they did every year on the plot they rented.

But Félix's thoughts, which were rather slow and simple, now jumped from one thing to another without apparent rhyme or reason. He suddenly remembered the words whispered by his mother at daybreak and felt an inner tremble, a heavy burden, then saw the stooping figure of his father walking with his gaze fixed on the ground, lost in thought. I don't understand, Félix thought, I just don't understand what is going on between them and how it has come to this, something everyone seems to have agreed is necessary. His 15-year-old mind found no way out and could not explain why it returned over and over again to images of childhood he thought he had forgotten. Like that time they had gone alone at the hour of the vertical sun to feel the soft breeze of the north wind under the shade of the *amate* tree that marked the spot of the old well, capped ages ago, and he, a boy of about seven, exploring the area while his father sat on a rock and took off his hat, had suddenly fallen into a narrow, black hole with coarse, damp walls that tore

From the Darkness

his desperate hands as he fell and grasped for something to hold on to. He remembered the blind seconds that only returned his hopeless calls until there, in the circle of sky that seemed to be closing in above him, was the silhouette of his father, the only one to hear his wailing, to console him with calm words, to run in search of something to save him from the foul-smelling swamp he had fallen into, to throw him a rope and pull with all his might to bring him back to a world that, for an instant, had seemed remote, foreign, like something lost forever.

Félix lifted his eyes and could see, over his father's head, the bottom of the pasture that descended to the *amate* and to the well he had just recalled, and the long shadows of the few trees that told him it was precisely five in the morning. The place grew light carelessly, as happens in fields of stubble where the weeds would not have been cleared all summer. Bartolo said nothing, he never did, but just drifted to the left looking for a mound of large, smooth, dark stones at the foot of a solitary low but leafy tree. There he put the food and the bag with the tools down carefully and ordered Félix to do the same with the gourd. That mound seemed more like an altar raised to some god, now abolished and cast into oblivion. Bartolo took out the rusty file he was carrying in his bag and silently began to sharpen the machete strung on his belt, staring intently at what he was doing, allowing himself to be embraced by the rustle of the leaves, the spirit of the morning dew. After a few minutes he stood up and told Félix to do the same with his machete, he should begin to weed from down there at the bottom of the field, he said... to here, and I want you to go along gathering the hay in piles to be burned another day when it has dried. Félix said yes, and watched his father walk away and grow smaller, his white shirt gleaming in the sun as he reached the other side, by the fence of another pasture, and began to stoop, delivering rhythmic blows with his machete.

This was the daily routine. They began work early to take advantage of the morning coolness, and took their first break at nine. But on this day there would be a variation, already announced: Mauricia would arrive to cut some tomatoes during those first few

Oswaldo Salazar

hours. Bartolo and Félix worked, seemingly heedless to this pending visit. It was not so for the women who had been left alone, face to face in the small space of the house.

The previous night, Rogelia had seen the little bottle containing pink liquid in Pedro's hands while he had explained to her how and why he had obtained it. And now that she was alone with her mother in the kitchen, the men having left while it was still dark, and her mother had taken refuge in her chores so as not to look her in the face, Rogelia was surprised to discover that same bottle, empty on the hearth, there for anyone to see. In that instant she understood it was for real, it was not a nightmare, and by now nobody could do anything about it. She got up and walked over to the hearth with the intention of examining the bottle, feeling it in her hands, smelling it, and was on the point of touching it when Mauricia suddenly came in, screwing up her face. Leave it, she said, don't touch that, I'll do everything, and she hurriedly snatched it up. Rogelia peered at her, trying to recognise her mother in the woman in front of her, and could feel her breathing, her pent-up strength. Don't look at me like that, she said after a moment, I'm doing this for everyone, for all of you, and for you above all. Rogelia did not answer, she was unable to. Mauricia added that sooner or later it had to happen and, she finished, only I have the guts to do it. The girl lowered her eyes, not daring to say a word, and her mother took the opportunity to take control of the situation and leave no possibility for rebellion or an utterance of guilt or regret. I'm waiting for a while, she said, but soon I'm going over there. I told Bartolo I'd go and cut some tomatoes and that's what I'm going to do. You're going to stay here and you're not going to budge until I get back, understand? Rogelia sat down without looking at her, waiting to see her thin silhouette leave through the doorway, and then to be left alone again.

Over the next half hour the two women criss-crossed past each other without saying a word as they negotiated the pathways of their daily duties and, when it was six-thirty, Mauricia said, I'm going, I don't know what time I'll get back, but wait for me as I told you to, and if anyone comes tell them where I've gone. She waited a

From the Darkness

few seconds until Rogelia said yes, as you wish, and then left by the kitchen door in the same direction as Bartolo and Félix.

Mauricia was thinking along the way that she would need to walk slowly, without doing anything strange, so as not to arouse suspicion, and she felt very curious about how, when, everything would unfold. Every now and again she looked around as if the stares of her neighbours were fingers tapping her on the back to ask what she was doing. But, remembering that Bartolo was an old stick-in-the mud about his routine, totally predictable and unlikely to surprise her, she calmed down. It's usually at about nine, she thought, never before then according to Félix, that he seeks out the gourd to refresh himself a bit. I have plenty of time to arrive and watch everything. She walked with small slow steps, her hands inside her shawl and her expression tense, uneasy, fixed on a route that she knew by heart. She reached the end of the street, at the edge of the town, and went the right way automatically, without even realising it. She was thinking about Félix, about the things he might have been imagining in that very same place just a few hours earlier. He was the one she was worried about, little Félix who, at the worst possible moment, had begun to identify with Bartolo and loved him, the poor innocent who didn't have a clue about what was happening, whom she didn't know how she would look in the eye again once it was all over.

She reached the paddock where the cattle were grazing and crossed the forest of coffee trees into the open where they were working. She saw them from afar, two small figures in motion as they cut the shrubs and, without moving and before they had become aware of her presence, she looked around and saw, hidden in the shade, the provisions, the clean clothes that they would put on at the end of the day and the gourd, shining like a polished stone. She decided to skirt around the field, and prayed they would not see her because she wanted to watch them unawares. On the other side of the fence she could move more freely, stealthily, all sight of her blocked. She approached them, found a bush big enough to hide behind, and waited, thinking, for a while. Bartolo, you old bastard, she said to herself with a frown as if remembering her whole life with him, blow by blow, more than 15 years without a blessed day of comfort and rest, whoever could see you there working would think you couldn't hurt a fly, but only I know you for what you are and I know that's not true. No-one can imagine what I've suffered and they wouldn't believe me if I told them. It would be useless. On the contrary, they'd tell me I'm an ingrate, that not only had you made me grow up, given me a house, a family, but that even now I'm still mucking about without appreciating everything I have.

Several minutes passed and the sun rose in the sky to its ephemeral throne with Mauricia leafing through the episodes and minutiae of her life while watching her husband and son as if she had nothing to do with them, as if it was possible to stand outside the current of events, at the margins of life, watching it pass by and resistant to the force of destiny.

Then suddenly her composure returned. Without thinking, she turned and walked into the field to look for the nicest tomatoes. She bent down where she saw the best and began to fill her basket. It would be past eight when she had finished. This was the moment to reveal herself. Perhaps it would make Bartolo and Félix bring forward their first break of the morning. She retraced her steps by the edge of the fence, no longer concerned that they would become aware of her. She walked, turning round every so often, and when she reached the corner where she had to turn left to get to the shaded rocks she saw that Félix had stopped working and was watching her silently, machete in hand. Moments later, removing his hat and drying the sweat with his arm, Bartolo also interrupted his work, seeing her for the first time since her arrival. As she sat just beside the gourd, Mauricia saw Bartolo speaking to his son and then returning to his work. Félix began to walk in her direction, downcast, more serious than usual.

"How is everything? Any problems?" asked Mauricia.

"No," said Félix, "same as ever."

"What did he say to you when he spoke to you just then?"

"Nothing, only to come over and see if you wanted something."

"Has he come over to drink any water? Have you noticed?"

"No, we've been working since we got here. Are you going to stay?"

From the Darkness

"Yes, and you get back over there, don't let him start wondering. I'm going to stay a bit longer, until you come over to refresh yourselves a bit."

"Okay, I have to go back to him."

"Yes, best go. And get rid of that face because you're going to make him nervous."

Alert, Félix retraced his steps. Mauricia watched him reach Bartolo. From there, everything seemed so peaceful – two men working in a field, stooped over the earth and, at the foot of the powerful mountains, unmovable since time immemorial, quiet in their indifferent slumber, the timid plantations and cottages scattered in their folds.

Every now and then Mauricia looked at the sky to work out the time, noticing how the transparent light and heat filled the air. There was not much time left, at any moment she would see Bartolo's silhouette standing upright and walking, head down, towards her. She wondered whether Félix, knowing everything, would come too, or if he would prefer to remain far off and not see anything. The machetes continued to glint in the sun as they were lifted to strike at the weeds. Mauricia listened in the distance and thought, in all that immensity, how insignificant their work was.

Nearly an hour had passed when she saw that Bartolo and Félix had stopped working and were heading towards her. It was nine in the morning. Her heart began to beat more forcefully and, although she could not see it, she felt a change in the expression on her face. Bartolo was walking ahead with a sombre expression and Félix, several steps behind, did not take his eyes off the ground. Weeks ago, Mauricia and Bartolo had become estranged, without violence, without reproach, and each now lived out their isolation by taking refuge in their chores, speaking only when necessary. Bartolo had acquired an air of resigned solitude, of a familiar failure to understand that he was ever further away from that indissoluble alliance between his wife and their children. This was how he felt as he reached the mound of stones where she was waiting.

"Did you manage to pick some tomatoes?"

Oswaldo Salazar

"Yes," she answered, lowering her gaze. "There were some ripe ones."

"The heat's beginning to intensify, that's why I like to take advantage of the morning coolness," he said, making a throwaway comment, removing his hat and putting it on the stones.

"I left Rogelia looking after the house," Mauricia said.

"Fine," he answered, sitting down a few steps away from her and getting ready to pick up the gourd, which had been in the shade.

During one of those silences in which all that could be heard was the wind swaying the branches of the trees, Félix, who did not say anything, saw a dog a few metres away. He fixed on it, losing himself in his thoughts for a few seconds, and realised that it was the mongrel belonging to Pedro Quezada, his father's enemy. He did not dare interrupt the conversation and thought he would mention it later, when they were returning from work.

"This water really is fresh," said Bartolo after drinking from the gourd. "Don't you want some?" he added, offering it to Félix.

"Don't worry," Mauricia said hurriedly, "I gave him some from mine when I came, you drink it, I have more here."

Bartolo did not answer, but continued to drink calmly, pausing to look at the distant landscape between gulps. Then he put the stopper in carefully, left the gourd in exactly the same place he had found it and, getting up, murmured to Felix to follow him.

Mauricia saw them head into the distance and although she was supposed to leave at any moment she could not resist the temptation to stay and wait for what was about to happen. She saw Félix speaking to his father while they were walking and him turning to point to something with his machete. Her heart missed a beat because she was afraid that, at any moment, Félix might betray her through fear, compassion or loyalty. Mauricia also turned to look, although there was nothing there. But after that she did not take her eyes off the pair as they moved away. She watched them stop, pick up the pitchforks they were also using, and begin working. But very soon Bartolo could clearly be heard coughing forcefully, as he did when he was drunk and it fell to her to clean up the vomit from the ground or the sheets where he was sleeping. Now, however, the

From the Darkness

man was groaning and in a loud voice, interrupted by the cough, he said something to Félix that she could not make out. Mauricia stood up and saw Félix helping his father walk towards her. On reaching her, Bartolo fell to his knees, moaning. Between muffled groans and curses, it seemed he was trying to say something. Mauricia bent down to help him but Bartolo was already on the ground, twisting and doubling up with pain. She wanted to know what he was trying to say and, in between his moans and groans, she moved closer to listen.

Félix, meanwhile, grabbed the gourd in an apparent fit of rage, beside himself, and, remembering what his mother had recommended several hours earlier, smashed it repeatedly against the stones until all that was left of it was a pile of pieces scattered in the weeds. Turning, he saw his mother kneeling on the ground and leaning towards his father who was now uttering something only she could hear.

Mauricia asked Félix to help. Each took an arm to carry Bartolo straight to town. After a few steps, he began to vomit with great force and Félix grew very scared when he saw the bloody streaks his father spat out. Bartolo fell to his knees again and this time they left him for a moment so that he could finish vomiting. It looked like he would bring up his guts through his mouth at any moment.

This was repeated many times on the journey. The paths of the forest seemed to go round in circles, like lost walkways with no direction. Bartolo was unable to stay on his feet and they carried him, nearly dragging him, with great difficulty. When they saw the first houses they felt relieved, the few people they came across asking what had happened, and them answering just that he was sick, they were going home and, please, call Doctor Rodríguez at the hospital and tell him to come at once because it was an emergency.

As they passed through the door, Félix dared to take a look at his father because he was moaning less, but he realised it was not because Bartolo was better. The poor man was exhausted, bathed in sweat, the colour of his skin had changed and his groans were softer, deeper. Félix thought this must have been like the shouts his father had heard from that well he had fallen into when he was a boy. Now it was Bartolo who was defenceless, pale and as cold as a corpse still hanging on to what little remained of life. But an infinite force was taking him and nothing could be done about it.

Rogelia met them with a look of fear that they had never seen before. She walked ahead of them, clearing the way right up to the bed. They could not agree whether to lay him down or to keep him sitting up so that he did not choke on the vomit that was by now just a yellow streak with red stains. They left him sitting, leaning against the wall, not daring to move him any more, as if aware that in his deathly pain he was drifting away from them and by now they would never be able to reach him. Only their glances surrounded him, in silence, motionless. Little by little, he doubled up on himself and leaned to his side until he was lying down with his feet dangling. Mauricia stood in front of him. Félix and Rogelia turned to look at her and, for the first time in their lives, felt the force, the unbreakable, triumphant willpower that now possessed her. I want you to go to the hospital, she told Rogelia, and to bring the doctor.

Minutes later, when only a rhythmic, languid and final moan could be heard, like the lament of a heart beating its last, Rogelia returned in a carriage accompanied by Doctor Raúl Rodríguez Padilla, director of the San Juan de Dios Hospital. Mauricia and Félix looked at each other for a second without saying anything until, with a firm movement of the head, she ordered him to go and meet the visitor with his shiny black case, whom everyone knew. The doctor appeared calm, with that characteristic expression he had shown in many difficult situations, a mixture of thoughtfulness and cold-bloodedness.

"Good day, doctor," said Mauricia, "come in."

"Good day," he answered. "What's going on here? Has Don Bartolo been taken a little ill on us?"

"Yes doctor," she said, "we think he's been poisoned."

"When did this crisis begin?" he asked, already kneeling beside Bartolo, examining his eyes, opening his mouth and taking his pulse.

From the Darkness

"Just over an hour ago, doctor."

"He's been vomiting a lot, I imagine?"

"Yes, since we left the place where they were."

"Do you have a sample?"

"Yes," answered Mauricia, showing him a white chamber pot she had under the bed.

On seeing it, Doctor Rodríguez Padilla's expression changed. He no longer seemed so full of confidence but was frowning and his expression betrayed concern.

"This man is on the verge of dying, he is bleeding inside. He must be taken to hospital immediately."

The doctor stood up and added that every second counted, that the patient would have to be taken in the carriage he had brought with him and that when they got to the hospital they would find him in the emergency room.

At eleven exactly, Bartolo entered the hospital and a team of two nurses and Doctor Rodríguez Padilla himself attended him to provide the urgent treatment he needed. Mauricia went with the doctor. Their children came a few minutes later and remained seated on the wooden benches in the waiting room, without talking, waiting for the storm of malicious questions from neighbours, friends, people they knew and, of course, the police commissioner. Mauricia took the chance to tell Félix and Rogelia not to say anything, she would answer the questions and all they had to do was back up what she said. They sat down. But they were tense, fearful when greeting the people who had hurried to the hospital for news and following the nurses who, every so often, left the room with rapid steps then re-entered hardly hearing those who asked: How is he? Do you think he's going to make it? Please, can you tell me what's happening? What does the doctor say? Can we speak with him? With a worried air, without even looking at them, the nurses replied: It's too soon, please wait, the patient is in a coma but stable. We're doing all that is humanly possible. Be patient.

Mauricia, for her part, fought off the questions of those who arrived in dribs and drabs. First came the neighbours who had found out when they had seen them carrying Bartolo back to the house, the very same people they had left snooping and commenting at their half-open door, stretching their necks and trying to imagine what had happened. Later, Bartolo's relatives arrived, his brother and his family, who had just found out and had come immediately.

Whoever could have seen her there, talking with one, then another, and at times with all of them at once, telling the same story over and over, would have said she was in complete control of the situation. And when the children came to tell her what the nurses had told them she whispered in their ears to remind them that they should say nothing.

After a while, when the visitors had dispersed through the corridors and patios of the hospital and begun to take their leave, Doctor Rodríguez Padilla appeared, tall and as calm as ever, in the doorway marked Emergency Service. Mauricia stood up and walked towards him mechanically. He was stable, the doctor said. Nothing more can be done. Now we must wait for the treatment we have given him to take effect. He was quiet for a moment without taking his eyes off her, and added: If you'll permit me, I have to go to my office. Mauricia lowered her gaze, turned back to the bench and sat down between her children.

It was the first time the doctor had looked at her carefully and he did not know what to think. There was her husband, in the emergency room, being destroyed inside because someone had poisoned him. And she would remain, shouldering the burden of her three children, without anyone to give her a hand.

But the young professional had been trained not to think in this way, and so decided to go to his office as soon as possible to draft the document that was now required. He walked along the upper corridor, painted in pale green, and arrived at an office in the middle of which stood a small, solitary desk and, on it, a shiny black typewriter. He sat down, took out a letterheaded sheet from the drawer to his right, slipped it into the roller, stopped for a moment to think, and finally wrote:

From the Darkness

Amatitlán, 15th of March 1939

Mr Justice of the Peace,
For your attention.

It is my humble duty to inform you that today at 11 o'clock the individual Bartolo García was admitted to the Emergency Service of this hospital showing symptoms of poisoning, his condition is grave, and I presume he is going to die.

Permit me to add that I have already sent a sample of his vomit to the Laboratory of the School of Pharmacology in Guatemala City to be analysed.

R. Rodríguez Padilla
Head Doctor

The letter was received at two forty-five in the afternoon by the secretary of the Amatitlán courthouse, the pupil lawyer Jorge Alcántara A. The judge and municipal intendant, Attorney Alberto Fuentes Novella, who had little to do and was ready to act on the smallest complaint that came through his door, decided to go to the hospital immediately to investigate what was happening. Judge and secretary left without delay and crossed through the lonely streets under the full weight of the afternoon sun.[2]

They arrived at five to three. Doctor Rodríguez Padilla went out to meet them and took them to his office where he ratified in full what he had sent in his alarming and prophetic note. With the firm intention of getting to the bottom of the matter, the judge then surprised his secretary when he said: Now all that remains is for us to interview this man and file a report about everything as we see it. But from what the doctor says this poor man won't be able to talk, noted the secretary. It doesn't matter, the judge replied, we have to get him on the record despite his condition.

They left the office and steered their way through the silence of the relatives and friends in the corridors until they reached the men's ward. Once you have seen him, we are going to move him, the doctor said, because there is no cure for this patient and other emergencies could come in. They walked between the patients ... *and in a bed* – Secretary Alcántara would write several minutes later, once back at the court – *was a man who showed symptoms of poisoning and in a state of agony, for which reason he could not respond to the questions asked of him by the undersigned Judge ...*

"What do you think, doctor?" the judge asked.

"It's only a question of hours," he replied.

"Okay, well, do what you have to and when you're ready send me your report. We'll be waiting."

Doctor Rodríguez Padilla bade them farewell and turned back to enter the ward. He did not want to repeat to the family what he had just told Judge Fuentes Novella. Bartolo was senseless, immobile. In a gesture of impotence as he stood beside the bed with his stethoscope hanging from his neck, the doctor put his hands in the pockets of his lab coat and, looking at the patient, realised he would never cease to be surprised or to feel something inexplicable when confronted by death. There's no training for this, he said to himself. He saw Bartolo's half-open mouth, out of which it seemed his life was now departing, his pallid colour, like a shroud that had emerged from within to envelop him, and he thought that within just a few moments he would have to go out and tell the family that he had died.

From the Darkness

II

She heard her mother calling with a suffocated, distant shout, appearing briefly at the window as usual to tell her that it was now late and she should come inside with her brothers to give a hand with the housework. She still had a few minutes more up there, she thought, perched in the tree that she considered her own and that she climbed to see, from on high, the roofs, the streets stretching out in the distance, and to imagine the soft, shining waves of the lake that seemed asleep under the midday sun.

She never acted on that first shout, waiting to hear the voice ordering her back again, this time stronger and more authoritarian: Mauricia, it's the second time I've had to call you, come here! Then she would begin her slow descent from the vantage point that allowed her to escape the small children, neighbours and relatives, and their boring games. She swung down from the branches as they became thicker until she was left hanging a metre from the ground, and jumped between the roots that spread out all around.

On that summer's day in 1921, like every Sunday, she had to interrupt the little ones' games, act like their mother and drop them off at their houses one by one until she was left alone, walking ahead, stopping every so often to wait for her little brothers who followed behind, laughing and protesting at having to go home.

At barely 12 years of age, Mauricia was already accustomed to domestic work. It had never seemed strange to her that she stayed

Oswaldo Salazar

in the house while her brothers went to school. Later, they would go to the countryside with their father and work the land and she would stay home, learning the job of housewife and waiting to be married in order to have her own house and children. Her earliest memories were of being beside her mother, hauling water, sweeping, washing dishes in the barrel or carrying a basket of clothes towards the lake. And they were not unhappy memories, on the contrary, this was her way of feeling part of the family. She also recalled that whole year during which she had had to go every day at first light to serve Madam Lucía Guzmán, the wife of Mr Bartolo García, a friend of her father's – the first time she had been away from home, she remembered well, and the only opportunity she had ever had to do something to alleviate the poverty, limitations and humiliation in which they lived.

We would never have been able to pay my father's debt, she repeated to herself, recalling the times she had been left alone with the man of the house, if I had not been going there, day after day, without complaining, without telling my mother anything out of fear of Don Bartolo.

Luckily, just a year after she started, when she had just turned nine, she had stopped going. Doña Lucía became gravely ill and her house fell into chaos. Don Bartolo and his son Lencho spent what they had in an effort to cure her, and abandoned the house in the last few days of her long agony. Mauricia had listened to her parents' comments: the poor Garciás, left alone, poor Lencho because Bartolo had taken to drinking, the poor boy did what he could but they lived like animals, why didn't Bartolo find a mother to look after the house and finish raising his son.

On that Sunday lunchtime, Mauricia did not imagine that everything she thought she had left behind would sweep her up again. She noticed, on entering last, after the boys, that her mother Arcadia was nervous. The table had not been set and on the hearth the logs had only just begun to burn underneath the terracotta pots. Nevertheless, her father Jacinto was seated in his place at the head of the table, very serious, and had been watching her since she had come through the door. Come, he said, I want to speak to you.

From the Darkness

Mauricia felt an emptiness in her stomach as she neared the table and pulled out a chair.

"Do you remember Bartolo García?" he said, the question being absurd.

Mauricia did not answer. She looked at him intently and, every few seconds, glanced at her mother wrapped in her shawl, standing silently behind him beside the adobe wall.

"It's just that one day this week he came to find me while I was sowing," Don Jacinto continued, looking worried. "He told me that little by little he had returned to a normal life, to working, to looking after his plot, and he had been able to save some money in the last two years. Let's say he brought me up to date with his life, because since Lucía died we haven't spoken at length due to everything that happened to him and his son Lencho. I knew all about this but anyway I let him speak because I realised he wanted to tell me something. He told me that his wife's sickness had left them in misery, that he had abandoned the planting when he turned to the drink, but that now he had regained his composure a bit and wanted to put his house in order. He asked about you, if you were working for a family or if you had gone to live with any man. I said no, that you still lived with us, but the time was coming, now you were a young woman and soon you would have to look for a husband and leave home. Then he smiled, he was happy, and he said he was in luck, and this was exactly what he had wanted to talk to me about. Mauricia, you will recall, has already worked in my house, he said, she knows us, even Lencho who is so shy showed her affection, and now that I am putting things in order I remembered her. Then he left me just looking at him in the face and went quiet for a moment. I'm not a man to beat about the bush, he continued, and what I want to ask you is whether you will give her to me so that she can live with me. I didn't know how to answer him, and I must have gone very serious because a little later he told me he knew he was very old for you, but he had savings and could leave you one of his properties, that we live nearby and have known each other for a long time, and we will always be able to see you and know how you are. I didn't answer him, I only told him to let me think about it.

Oswaldo Salazar

Then he went and I've not seen him since."

Mauricia listened without knowing what to think. She knew her father never consulted anyone or discussed anything but only gave orders. So it could only be one of two things, either he had decided to say no to Bartolo, in which case there would be no sense telling her all this or, more likely, he had thought yes, it was good for her to join that old man in order to safeguard her future, and he was just informing her.

"But I've been thinking since then," he continued, "day and night, not only about you, but about everybody, about our situation, above all about the brothers who've come after you, and every day it's more difficult to feed them. So last night I made my decision. Tomorrow you will go and live with him. It's what's best for everyone, you more than anyone because Bartolo is a mature man, established; moreover, we know him and we know he is a good person. I'm sure that right at this moment he's not thinking of marriage but with time he will, and he's not so old that you can't have children with him."

Mauricia looked at Doña Arcadia, her mother, who had not raised her eyes from the ground and was listening to her husband's every word. It was too late. There was no longer time to speak out, to tell them the things that Mr Bartolo had said when he was left alone with her, the way he had touched her legs and opened her blouse and run his thick, rough fingers over her tender chest, tense with fear. It was useless to tell them that this man frightened her, this old man who had said things to her that she could not understand, and had always ended up looking her in the eyes and pointing with his finger while saying: Remember, this is a secret, Jacinto and Arcadia must not find out because they would be very angry with you.

"Your father's right," her mother said suddenly, and Mauricia noticed she was crying, "he told me this morning and I also think this is the best thing for you. Sooner or later you're going to have to do this and it's better with a grown man we know, who's going to look after you and is not to going to take you to live who knows where."

From the Darkness

Mauricia wondered why she had not told her parents about Mr Bartolo at the time, what had stopped her. And now... now that I have to be his woman, now that he's waiting for me, what's all this about having a husband and, moreover, a stepson who is nearly my age? At home with her parents, although just for a few moments, she had time to play, to go out and run with her little brothers and climb the tree, but in that house where, she remembered, they put her to work all day, she would not be able to and would spend the whole time shut indoors, like her mother who only went out to the market and the tortilla grinder once a week.

"In the afternoon," her father said without waiting for a reply, "after lunch, I'm going to look for him at his house to tell him what I've decided and, if he's in agreement, tomorrow when I've returned from work we're going to take you."

Mauricia would never forget that Monday afternoon which she spent arranging her clothes and preparing for a journey she knew had no return. Doña Arcadia helped her without saying a word, in silence, as if she knew that even in his absence the father would be listening to what she said and watching her every movement. They finished before they had to, and sat down to wait. Their silence that afternoon was their way of waiting. Mauricia knew all the sounds of the house, she knew the hours that the neighbours kept, those who passed by and knocked on the door and, above all, she knew by heart when and how her father would arrive home, from his careful footsteps to the soft way he removed the bar of the door and walked across the patio before appearing in the doorway of the room where they ate.

That afternoon, Don Jacinto did not change his Monday routine at all and appeared in the doorway at the usual time, not to eat but to take her by the hand and give her over to the man with whom she would spend the rest of her life. They walked through the same old streets, she and her father in front and her mother a few steps behind, but no matter how hard she tried, Mauricia could not remember this journey years later when she was telling the story to her daughter Rogelia in an effort to show her what men are really like, even resorting at times to explaining about them from books.

Oswaldo Salazar

Yes, she remembered vividly the wait at the dining room table and, of course, the moment when her father knocked at the Garcías' door that she knew so well. But she had erased the journey itself from her memory. It was as if one moment she was still in the house helping her mother and the next she had found herself in the room of a stranger, rigid with fear, quietly awaiting his pleasure.

Bartolo received them happily, invited them to enter, but her father did not wish to go through the door. Instantly, he handed her over. Mauricia crossed the threshold and saw her parents from inside while she heard, as if in a dream, the recommendations of her father, who did not dare look her in the eyes or even say goodbye. Nor was her mother, poor thing with her white skirt and laced blouse, capable of raising her eyes to look at her for the last time from the other side of the doorway.

From that moment on, I remember everything, she said assuredly to Rogelia, who listened almost without breathing, from the moment the light from the street was extinguished as Bartolo shut the door and we were left alone and Lencho looked at us without saying anything. It was time to eat, I remember as if reliving it, Mauricia recalled as if she had stayed there frozen in time and someone else had carried on living in her place. Bartolo told me to go to the room, he said I already knew which one, and to leave my things there and come and heat up the food. I did so, only this time when I went in I felt something strange, as if at any moment I would hear the voice of the dead Lucía, I felt her watching me everywhere as if she had been incorporated in the unmade bed with her long tangled black hair all over her face. I left my bag of clothes and ran out. Bartolo and Lencho were at the table waiting for me with empty bowls. So then I went to the hearth, which had been lit, and I heated beans, tortillas, and made them coffee. For the first time I sat with them and they spoke about work as if I wasn't there. From time to time they looked at me to ask me for something and I got up without saying anything and returned with what they wanted, until Bartolo put his coffee cup on the table with a thud and told me to clear everything up and then come and sleep with him.

That was my first day in the house, she told Rogelia. Some

From the Darkness

months later you were born and then your brother and even Manuela sneaked her way out, and 20 years have gone by just like that. Rogelia had heard the story countless times and Mauricia always asked at the end: we're almost sisters, don't you think? And she laughed with a kind of complicity that frightened her daughter.

What Mauricia did not recount, and what Rogelia did not dare to ask about, is what had happened the moment she entered the bedroom and encountered Bartolo, naked from the waist up, waiting for her. He told her not to stand there as if made of wood, not to be frightened and to come close, that he would not harm her. And she walked over with slow, small steps, around the bed, until reaching his outstretched arms that he had extended to take her by the waist and bring her closer until she was between his open legs. Then those rough hands, that her little girl's body already knew, lowered themselves down to her unformed hips and her trembling legs, went beneath her skirt and began to rise slowly while Bartolo closed his eyes, making Mauricia think that men must shut their eyes when they are touching because, in fact, they are holding their eyes in their hands.

Rogelia would never find out from Mauricia's lips that Bartolo had not wanted to listen to her weeping, her pleas for him not to do that, for her very life, because it scared her – that without responding, breathing in her ear, he had positioned himself in order to sit her on the bed yet be able to remove his trousers and underpants. How could she tell her daughter that it was in this moment that she saw that dark, menacing, blind monster that made her recall a smell she had already experienced once and, vainly, had tried to forget? And if, in any case, one day Rogelia dared to become curious, Mauricia, indignant, would tell her not to poke her nose in, to be respectful. But this was such a personal thing that even she did not want to revisit those images that assaulted her from time to time on summer nights, bringing with them the perverse smile of this unknown man who told her you are not going to call me 'Don' Bartolo now that I'm your husband and you my little woman, then put his knee on the ground in order to lower zippers, open buttons and slide off her garments, which fell as if they were soft green leaves torn from the tree by light rain and the first wind.

No, it was not possible, her daughter had the right to another destiny and must never find out that, now naked and lying on the bed, her hands had not even been able to cover up her body as it bristled with fear, that her final defence had been to resist the force of this big man as he separated her legs to steer the blind monster into the depths of pain; that at first, even with all the force of a peasant, it had been hard for him; and that she saw no more because she had covered her face as she felt the pounding becoming deeper and not stopping until Bartolo, beaded with sweat, had fallen upon her, groaning as if someone was torturing him and calling her names she had never heard before.

Rogelia would stay on the straight and narrow, Mauricia thought, and thank God she had met Pedro, a docile and caring boy, not like that brute Bartolo. From the letters he had written about that famous debt, one could see that he was decent and respectful, and that he was mad about her daughter. This was what was most important and to keep it thus Mauricia was prepared to suppress her own memories, to paint for Rogelia a rose-tinted landscape of intimacy and, only for her, to subdue the demons that haunted her. Those from the past, of course, but also those of the future – the desire she felt at times, like a burning in the middle of her chest, to live alone, to be in charge of her own affairs and not to have to say yes just because Bartolo wanted her to, to be able to choose for once in her life and not be held accountable to anyone, but above all to live without fear, without anxiety, without the distress that she had felt ever since that Monday afternoon when she had seen her parents depart and leave her at the mercy of Bartolo and his son Lencho.

But it was becoming increasingly difficult to pretend nothing was going on because children are curious and youths even more so. They are always asking questions, inquiring, conjecturing, and it is better to tell them the truth because they can smell lies. Rogelia, for example, when she had turned into a young woman of the same age as Mauricia had been when she had gone to live with Bartolo, began

From the Darkness

to ask questions, and Mauricia had told her that she was still too young. But at my age you... , the girl replied, and Mauricia had not let her finish. Yes, she said, but you can't use my life as an example, I don't want you to go through the same, you have to look after yourself and give things time, find yourself a good man and get married. Imagine, she would continue, that at your age I was expecting you and, during those first few months, which were eternal, at times lonely, waiting for your father to come back in the early hours I turned in the bed and felt you growing here inside and I cried, I cried every night for my parents, for a home that now seemed in another world. I wanted to see my mother and hug her and hear her tell me it wasn't really happening, it was all only a bad dream and I should go back to sleep. Life is hard, my girl, it's difficult to get used to dreams from which one never wakes. But time erases everything, life goes on and there is no way out – it has to be confronted.

The first ten years were the most difficult, she had told her children a thousand times, and above all Félix who listened to everything without saying a word. I had you, and while I was expecting one I had to bring up the other and, moreover, look after the house and put up with your father and Lencho. Yes, Uncle Lencho, as you called him, but who was really your half brother.

She was talking about Florencio García Guzmán, the legitimate son of Bartolo and his wife Lucía, who was nearly the same age as Mauricia and who had died years ago and was now remembered by nobody. Poor boy, Mauricia said with an air of false nostalgia, he died before his time.

At this point of the story, Rogelia always asked to hear what it had been like, because they were little then and now could not remember. Mauricia lowered her voice and recounted how everything had begun very early on the 3rd of May 1929, the very day of the Amatitlán festival. You father was not going to work that day and had been on a binge since the night before. Lencho, by contrast, was getting up early because he liked to go to the church to see the preparations for the festival of Infant Jesus. When he got up, I served him a plate of beans and he went into the street. You have seen what this is like, it's a pilgrimage to the church, no-one stays at home. Lencho left with everybody else but came back soon after. He was pale, sweating, and couldn't stop spitting out yellow bile because by now he had nothing in his stomach. So I laid him down and went to tell Bartolo to look at him. The kid was all curled up in bed, wailing and saying he was dying. Your father sent me to the hospital and I went running, but on the way I asked myself what was I going to say to him if I couldn't find anyone? Sure enough, I arrived and there wasn't a soul there, it was deserted, and I just spoke with a nurse who told me she couldn't budge because of the patients she was looking after and either I followed the procession to see if I could find the doctor, or better still brought the sick child to the hospital and waited to see what time people returned from the festival.

At this point Mauricia paused to explain that while she was speaking to the nurse she could hear in the distance the hullabaloo of the procession, the bangers and rockets set off on street corners when the icon of the little boy passed by with his expression of compassion, seated on his throne, blessing the people with his plump little hand. Then I returned, she continued, and Bartolo was desperate, he had gone to knock at the neighbours' to seek help, but no-one had opened the door. They were all out. When he saw me, he ran over and grabbed me by the shoulders and I had to tell him I hadn't found anyone, and that if we took him it would be pointless because we'd only be sitting waiting, and perhaps it was better to look after him in the house and not move him because, the poor thing, you should've seen him, now had no strength, like a chick lying there with the chamber pot at his side. He was no longer screaming, just quiet, as if he was going and this was his farewell. I did everything, I gave him hot water, cornflour drink, to see if he could keep something down. But it was impossible, he threw everything up as soon as he had been given it. After that, he had no strength left even to swallow, and fell asleep. In that moment, kneeling as I was at the edge of the bed, I turned to look at Bartolo, and told him we should let him rest, and perhaps now that he had calmed down he needed to sleep, regain his strength, and when he woke up we could try to see if he wanted anything. We stayed there,

From the Darkness

keeping watch over him, without speaking and listening to his breathing, that was at times agitated. And down below, when night was already falling, the rockets and bangers began exploding in the sky again. It was the Infant Jesus returning to the church. Bartolo had not moved from Lencho's side for one moment. He didn't want to eat or rest the whole day, which he spent talking to Lencho between tears as he held his feeble hand. Then I had to go to my parents' house to pick up you and Félix, it was by now night-time, and when I came back I asked him how Lencho was. And in a broken voice, without turning to look at me, he told me he'd gone, his son was dead and nothing could be done. I think it's the only time I've ever seen Bartolo cry, Mauricia finished by saying. And the children moaned about not having been there to witness something they could only imagine through their mother's story.

Rogelia and Félix had heard this tale many times without knowing for sure whether their mother added or removed bits or whether her imagination was changing the facts to suit the form and convenience of her fantasies. Then, as soon as they had put her in a good mood, they went back to demanding she tell them how everything had begun. Ever since her fiancé had come along it had puzzled Rogelia, the eldest, that her father had never recognised her as a daughter. On several occasions Mauricia had had to weather the storm of these doubts. But on the 15th of February, a month before her father's death, after doing her morning chores and errands and filled with courage, perhaps egged on by Pedro, Rogelia sat down in the kitchen to wait for Mauricia to have a bit of time so she could put her on the spot and ask her, pleading with all her life, to explain what exactly had happened, because you know I can't talk to him. Mauricia, agitated without knowing whether from happiness or an attack of anguish, had noted upon entering that, whatever it was her daughter wanted to bring into the open, now there was no way out. She listened attentively and calmed down when she had verified that her daughter did not know she was going out, least of all where. Then, possessed of a whiff of courage, she said that's fine, you're a big girl now, and if I tell you it's so you don't have to go through the same thing. You were born just nine months after your father and I began to live together and, as you will have to learn in life, my poor little girl, an old man, no matter how good he is, never, and listen carefully to what I am telling you, never will confide in a youngster. It makes them fear they are not real men. And then, even with the bill of sale in their hands, they keep seeing things that are not there. And that bastard of a father of yours was the same. I was still there washed out on the bed the day after you were born when he appeared with a long face and told me that he had already been to the registry office and had registered you under my name only. What was he thinking? That my Uncle Chinto had given me the child? I don't know. In life you judge others by your own actions. And you?, Mauricia asked after a pause, why all these thoughts? I don't know, replied Rogelia, everything is so mixed up. Sometimes I can't sleep or I wake up and think things. Don't think nonsense, said Mauricia categorically, better still, run an errand for me: I want you to go and buy some bread, but not here in the neighbourhood at Don Luis's. At the shop in the park.

Reprimanding her daughter had given her peace of mind. Mauricia watched Rogelia go out through the door and felt the relief of being alone for a while. She had to get her thoughts in order and erase any trace of suspicion from the way she was behaving. She still had a few minutes in which to take a bath before leaving for the appointment that had made her so nervous. Hurriedly, she entered her room and set herself to tidying up the mess so that when Rogelia returned everything would seem normal. She did it without thinking, as she did every day. When she was ready, she went to the wardrobe to look for the clothes she was going to wear and, seeing herself in the mirror, stopped for a moment. She looked at her eyes carefully. Was it obvious? Was she the same Mauricia who had left in the morning? From now on, things would never be the same, she thought. Then she crossed her arms behind her back, slowly, feeling for the buttons of her blouse. She undid them one by one, nonchalantly, without caring about what she was doing, until she had removed the garment completely, revealing a slim torso and a white brassiere. She lowered her head and undid the sash that kept up her long, wide skirt and with the same lack of interest she let it fall

From the Darkness

to the floor then, without removing her shoes, stepped out of it. She bent down to pick it up and walked a few steps to the wardrobe, put her clothes away and took off her underwear there, in front of the stained mirror on the wardrobe door. It reflected tender breasts with dark nipples, a slender waist and round, firm hips, appropriate for her young age. For a moment, Mauricia looked at her body. Then she lifted her hands and put them beneath her breasts, lifting them a little. She began to lower her hands slowly across the bristling surface of her skin. She encircled her belly and, in a slow movement, finally, her hands stopped there, pressing tenderly. She thought about Hilario, in the dark house where he had taken her the first time they had been together and where, surely, they would always return when they were ready to be alone in the bed with no headboard in a corner beside a chair. She could feel again how he had taken her hand and together they had crossed through the darkness, and how, once on the bed, he had sat her on his legs. Mauricia could not avoid remembering her feet hanging like those of an inert, defenceless, ventriloquist's dummy at the mercy of his caprices as he takes all its weight and moves it at his pleasure.

Soon she regained her composure and, thinking she must be wasting time, became anxious. She did not want Rogelia to come back and find her still there, delayed, running about as ever doing daily chores. Yet while she finished choosing clothes she congratulated herself for having sent Rogelia out to the park, not only giving her time to do what she needed and to leave without anyone seeing her or asking where she was going or even how long she would be, but also because that way she had kept herself away from the watchful eyes of her neighbours.

When Rogelia had asked why she had to shop so far away if Don Luis's bakery was local, Mauricia had told her she didn't like his bread and it didn't cost anything to go further, and the girl had lowered her eyes and gone ahead without protesting. But the truth was that since Mauricia had gone to live with Bartolo she had preferred, perhaps instinctively, to keep her distance from the neighbours. Yes, from all those old crocks who had been friends of the late Lucía, her boss and Bartolo's first wife, who looked down on her as if she

Oswaldo Salazar

were a servant recently arrived from the Calderas hamlet and who, at the end of the day, had been left with the house and the husband of the lady who had given her work and, above all, taken her into her confidence. Poor Lucía, they told Mauricia that it was being rumoured, she had endured so many sacrifices and limitations all her life to get her own little house and now this so and so is left with everything. No-one knows whom she really works for. But when they recounted these rumours, they never said who had started them and that was why she had no faith in any of them, without exception. In Luis Lezana, the baker, and his wife; in Federico de León, who lived next door and whom she imagined was always pressing his ear up against the wall to hear what was happening on the other side; in Candelaria Pérez, the old spinster who was not even from Amatitlán and was given to snooping and judging everyone else's business; in Julián Calderón, Bartolo's friend who, like him, worked the land and had been his confidant since before she had known him; and in Rosalía Diéguez, the widow who had been a close friend of the late Lucía. Above all, the person she had least confidence in was Alberto Aquino Morán, Bartolo's first cousin, a farmer like him, who had envied him all his life and who, at least while her husband was out, never hid how much he desired her for being young and pretty, and took the liberty of saying that she couldn't fool him, he knew exactly who she was and if he had more money than Bartolo she would come to live with him. He always finished by saying that one day, sooner or later, she was going to be his and to remember his words because when she least expected it, at any careless moment, he was going to take the opportunity to have his way with her. Mauricia despised him deeply, but tried not to show it, especially in front of Bartolo. She did not want to create problems where she would be the main loser. She did not trust Bartolo. She had never felt secure with him. She was convinced that for many reasons – age, family, gender – when the time came and when dealing with a relative and, moreover, a man, Bartolo would not take her side. He had never been committed to her and, truth be told, nor her to him. She had thought a thousand times that if one day Alberto Aquino took a liberty, she would keep quiet, she would

From the Darkness

have to, there would be no other way. So it was a simple matter, she could only defend herself by keeping her distance, by not becoming close to him or his family.

But over the years this attitude had generated resentment in everyone around her – the rancour of the deaf, of those who only muttered sullenly from between clenched teeth. Mauricia knew this and it did not bother her, on the contrary, she was prepared to pay a price like that to isolate herself and her children. Over time, she dreamed, she would be repaid. She did not know how, but she clung to the hope that a time would come when she would be accountable to no-one and could do as she pleased with the house, the money and her time.

Mauricia had finished bathing and now she was making herself up in front of the mirror. Suddenly she felt anxious that she might forget and leave out, for Bartolo or any of the children to see, the letter she had received that week and now had to carry around with her at all times. She ran to the chest of drawers to fetch it and keep it safe, close to her bosom. As she did so, she looked up and smiled. It was a smirk of complicity with herself, and she looked towards the street and remembered the moment when Hilario had pulled out from his bag the letter that was now between her breasts and told her that he had never been good at talking, that sometimes it was better to write down one's feelings so the recipient could read what the heart dictated, calmly and as many times as she wished. She had certainly read it many times and could remember phrases, entire paragraphs, without effort, almost mechanically, as if it were a voice coming from within.

The letter was simple, explanatory, it bore all the hallmarks of a tired man long alone who confused custom with resignation and who, suddenly, perhaps too late, is filled with illusions and then pauses along the way to try to understand, to ask himself if what's happening is real or just one more mirage in the desert of old age. He had written it in solitude, struggling with himself, sensing that he was leaving all the gravity of his well and truly lived 55 years of age exposed. But also, as he had proceeded, he had become convinced that he could not stop, as if with this he would be paying off a personal debt after a whole life of denial and renunciation.

Although the words and the writing did not come easily to a man accustomed only to working the land, during the days that this process took Hilario felt as if the words were his own life, that they rose up from an unknown fountain and some of them called to the others until completing a timid, sincere confession that, in its final form, read:

Guatemala, January 1939

Mrs Mauricia Hernández U.
For your attention.

Esteemed Madam,

It is with great embarrassment and fear that I have dared to write these sincere words with the objective of making you aware of how much I have been thinking about our incipient relationship. So, after thinking about this a great deal, I am putting pen to paper to provide you with written proof of what I told you that first day I dared to express my feelings to you. And you were not to know and I shouldn't tell you this, but when a man gets close to a woman, please believe me, he must vanquish that nagging fear of rejection. It's true, although it may appear to be or is expressed as the contrary. And my situation, as you know, is more serious because of the number of years between us. However, that did not stop you entering my dreams from the moment Bartolo made you his, and little by little you turned into a young woman. For this reason, what has happened in the last few days is for me the realisation of a dream, of something impossible. Imagine, at my age, and given the distance from women that I have lived in for years, the fact that you would have smiled at me, with you being so famous for being unfriendly and for not speaking to anybody, was a real miracle. In that moment I told myself, Hilario, you're a slug if you don't take advantage of the opportunity that Mauricia who knows nothing

From the Darkness

about your life is giving you. Thus it was that Sunday, on passing each other by, I told you how lucky it was for me to run into you and to be able to greet you. You only smiled as if my words had scared you. I swear, I had not thought of anything in advance, it came out spontaneously, as they say, because of the sheer pleasure of seeing you. And so it all began. Here inside, in my breast, suddenly grew a hope, a happiness which I don't need to tell you about, as if I was young again and now I was not thinking of anything else (work, the house, the journeys) but seeing you again and giving you news of my affections. At times I thought, hold on a moment, take care, remember that you are already old and you are only going to scare her off with this emotion, let her seek you out. But I could not, I abandoned myself to my feelings and waited with yearning for the moment that I would see you again to tell you everything, not only the pretty things but also my fears, my anguish about seeing you in the arms of another man. Yes don't think I'm not aware, that I'm deaf or blind to what I see or what is said around me, and that I don't realise how many want you to notice them. Perhaps I will never forgive myself for what I am going to confess to you, but I am jealous even of Pedro García, that youngster who is the betrothed of your daughter and who enters your house every day and can talk to you without anyone thinking anything about it. Love also brings sorrow and doubts and I, with you there far away and now reading this letter, am living both sides of this coin. But since our first encounter the other day I have been more at peace. Thank you, thank you very much for the proof you gave me by letting yourself be taken by the hand where I wanted to take you. I still have the sensation of your presence, of your docile silence whilst we were getting close to each other at my house and when I had still not told you anything about my intentions. I still feel your hand in mine as I was guiding you through the darkness to take you to the bed. You said nothing to me, as if expecting this in advance, you did not put up the slightest resistance and, you are not going to believe me, this doubled my yearning to consummate our love. For this reason when I had you in front of me ready for whatever was my will, I desisted. And I did

Oswaldo Salazar

so to demonstrate to you that this wasn't all I was looking for with you. Or perhaps yes, I don't know, the thing is at that moment I changed my mind, on feeling the warmth of your skin on my hands while my eyes were adapting to the darkness and little by little you began to appear to me as if I was seeing you for the very first time. It was a revelation that has given me much to think about.

Perhaps this has no sense, and please do not think me mad but I have come to believe that our encounter made me realise I was living in the shadows, blind, that I have lived my entire life in such a way. But now with you at my side things are no longer the same, as if a tiny little light, twinkling there in the distance, had been lit in order to illuminate the dense shadows, the source of my fear.

God knows what you are thinking now because I didn't want to touch you. It was to guard this small flame and not let it go out.

I'm getting to the end and feel I haven't written what I wanted to. Well, would it have been sensible to expect anything else?

Now I have to say farewell, or rather to say see you soon, until the longed-for moment of our next encounter, here by my side, where there will be no dawn if you, dear Mauricia, do not show up. With the affection of a devoted admirer,

Hilario A.

Mauricia, now ready to leave, touched the letter to her breast and smiled. She could not leave it there, lying around. Moreover, she would ask Hilario to read her extracts and he was going to have to conquer his timidity, that fear of ridicule all old men have. She calculated the time that it would take for Rogelia to return from the park. When she realised she had time to spare to go through everything once more and leave nothing to chance, then depart without bumping into her by the house, she relaxed. She also thought that the neighbours would be eating and those accustomed to going home at lunch time would not yet have arrived from work. She looked at herself in the mirror for the last time and had a fleeting sensation that her reflection did not belong to her, as if another woman inside it was looking at her with her eyes. But without stop-

From the Darkness

ping to think, she turned and walked to the door. As she shut it behind her, she felt the burning summer heat that immersed her entirely in its steamy humidity and claimed every centimetre of her skin.

From the Darkness

III

Doctor Raúl Rodríguez Padilla had returned from his rounds when he noticed vomit seeping gently from Bartolo's half-open mouth. It was like a last breath, the final gesture of a vanquished body. Quickly, as if still treating an emergency, the doctor straightened the patient's head and opened his eyelids. There again was that look he had seen so many times, without light, without an object, utterly useless. He then took the pulse on the neck and confirmed that the heart had stopped beating. He looked at his watch: it was four-twenty in the afternoon.

Outside, seated in silence on the wooden benches, remained only the immediate family. Now came the part the doctor hated most, going out to confront their hopes, their anxieties, and having to say the absurd, that the patient was no more, that he had gone and there inside, behind those doors, was only a corpse and, moreover, that one of them would have to go and identify it, as if it were someone else, an unknown harbinger of pain. But it was not the first time the young doctor from the capital had done this, so he told a nurse to cover Bartolo with the sheet and take him to the autopsy room while he would take the family to his office. Get someone to help you, he said, and I'll catch up in a moment.

He opened the door of the men's ward and immediately found himself under the relatives' watchful eyes. They were all there, the wife and the two grown children, waiting in the wide corridor leading to the inner garden. He walked across to them, as they stood up, and said: Can you accompany me to the office, please? They walked in silence along the upper corridor, the doctor ahead of them. When they reached the office, and without inviting them to sit, Doctor Rodríguez Padilla told them without further ado that Bartolo had died, that everything possible had been done, but these efforts had been in vain because it had taken so long to provide treatment for the now deceased patient and he had consequently suffered grave, irreparable damage to his digestive system. The doctor paused, taking refuge behind his desk as if it were a trench in a war zone. There was a moment's silence. Rogelia began to sob gently, repressing her tears. Félix did not lift his eyes from the ground. Mauricia was the first to react. And now what, doctor? she asked with a rigid, impenetrable expression. For the first time the doctor felt the woman's strength. Now, he said, still disturbed, you or another relative have to accompany me to the autopsy hall to identify the body. Afterwards, I shall stay there to make ready for the autopsy first thing tomorrow, and at ten, he said, looking at his watch, you can come for the body.

The doctor walked to the door and opened it. Mauricia gestured with authority to her children to move out of the way and, decisively, walked behind the doctor. As they passed the casualty waiting room, she ordered them to wait for her there. Now alone with the doctor, she continued her journey between the high columns, passing through doors, crossing wards of men and women who gaped at her in surprise from their sickness and pain, from the solitude felt by someone who alone knows their sorrow. They came out on to the patio beside the autopsy hall and Mauricia could not avoid reading the words written on the wall, by hand, in trembling strokes:

FOR TO BE CARNALLY MINDED IS DEATH; BUT TO BE SPIRITUALLY MINDED IS LIFE AND PEACE Rm 8:6

Quickly, after having crossed the wide open space, the doctor pushed the last door open to reveal a blinding light. He did not need to say anything. It was the autopsy hall and, at its centre, small and wrapped in a dirty and creased sheet, was a body, a simple inert

From the Darkness

body watched over by two orderlies who observed Mauricia with a fixed stare and without moving a muscle in their faces. Doctor Rodríguez Padilla went forward while she walked carefully, as if in a minefield. It is a mere formality, he told her, but we have to do it, and he lifted the sheet revealing a pallid face consumed by pain, covered with a viscous film that made it seem like a wax doll, not of this world. Mauricia looked at it and said without thinking, yes, it's him, my husband Bartolo – but inside she thought, no, what was before her, completely incapable of listening, of responding, was not Bartolo, and that she had never seen that expression, that grimace of abandon and infinite distance.

Well, the doctor said, interrupting her thoughts, please leave us alone now and return later at the time I told you to. Mauricia lowered her eyes, turned, and left without a word. Now she had to pick up her children, go to the house and do one last thing before the hours of insomnia that lay ahead.

In the meantime, the doctor and his team, with everything now prepared for the post mortem examination – scalpels, scissors, saw and the rest of the instruments – shut the room, leaving the body alone, immobile, waiting for the moment when it would reveal the cause of its death. These cases were not common in a small town like Amatitlán. But because of the gravity of a case that surely concealed a criminal mystery, the doctor thought it best to proceed as soon as possible and with all the professionalism and objectivity that his science afforded.

Mauricia, Rogelia and Félix returned home to change and eat something. Mauricia took the opportunity to tell her children that the doctor had told her they had to go and collect the body the next day at ten. First, she told them, we have to run some errands and later we shall go to the hospital and collect your father. They did not ask what she meant and continued to eat in silence.

At around seven in the evening, after stopping off at the funeral parlour to order a casket and ask them to send it to the hospital at ten the next morning, they arrived at the half-open doors of the police station to make a formal complaint about the death of Bartolo García Morán.

Oswaldo Salazar

The police commissioner, Francisco Flores G., received them cordially in a ramshackle office, standing behind an old desk untidily covered with papers. He was not a man who dealt with things delicately, it should be said. Rather, he was rough and simple, but keen and obsessive when it came to carrying out his duties. Moreover, so the women said, he was always falling for someone. It was no secret to Mauricia that the commissioner had had his eye on her for a while. He had repeatedly sought an opportunity to talk to her and, between jokes, to insinuate how much her figure, her laugh and her way of walking attracted him.

That evening, Commissioner Flores, as they called him in the town, could not get over how late it was for such a visit, and a flicker of disappointment crossed his face when, just behind Mauricia, in trooped her two children. Rogelia and Félix, aged 18 and 16 respectively, as he would write the following day in dispatch number 273 that he would send to the justice of the peace to bring to his honour's attention the purpose of Mrs Hernández Urbina's surprise appearance.

Mauricia's tale was direct and concise, and the commissioner tried to transcribe it thus, relying on his memory. Truth be told, despite his experience, the story had moved him. It is not every day that a healthy and upright man, as Bartolo appeared to be, is jolted out of his routine and within twenty four hours is, as they say, dead and buried. Particularly impressed on his memory was the way Mauricia detailed the time and specific circumstances of what had happened. For example, that Bartolo and Félix, on arriving at the plot they leased from Don Emilio Barrera, had left the gourd beside a pile of stones then gone from it a distance of approximately one hundred metres, losing sight of it because of the weeds; and that at half past seven the claimant had reached, with the aim of cutting tomatoes, a position about eighty metres from the gourd; and that at about several minutes past nine the aforementioned common-law husband had gone to the gourd and taken some gulps of water; and that within a short while he had headed violently to where she was, dragging the gourd with him, and indicated that he felt a strong pain in the stomach and his whole body felt disturbed, telling her:

From the Darkness

"*My girl, that damned Pedro Quezada has finally fulfilled his threats to kill me, there's no doubt that while Félix and I were getting on with our work, that man crept up on the gourd and poisoned the water because, when I drank it, it seemed pungent and slightly sweet and had a strange smell, and I can assure you it was him because at half past eight I saw Pedro's dark dog near the gourd.*" She recounted, moreover, the burden they had then endured trying to save Bartolo's life and that, despite the efforts of Doctor Rodríguez Padilla, it had all been in vain and when all was said and done her common-law husband had died that afternoon. Consequently, she had come to him to request the arrest of the aforementioned Pedro Quezada Morales, given that she also had evidence he had sworn, in some way, that he would have to kill her common-law husband.

This was why, immediately fulfilling his duty, Commissioner Flores had ordered without further delay the arrest of the accused whom, he told the judge, you will permit me to put at your disposal in the prison cells of this city.

But the commissioner's diligence had not been limited to capturing Pedro Quezada on the word of Mauricia. No. He had tried to corroborate the story and he had questioned the minor Félix Hernández, along with his mother the only witness, then and there, about the events referred to in the complaint. The youth confirmed his mother's every word, passively. What's more, he added that he could confirm *having himself seen the dog that had approached the gourd and that he recognised the bitch as the aforementioned Quezada's property*.

When it came to her turn, Rogelia, who had remained quiet, limited herself to declaring only that s*he could confirm that her father returned from the fields in a state of agony and so the doctor was called, and he ordered him to be admitted to hospital because* (and this was what was most important about her testimony) *according to him, they were dealing with a poisoning.*

Not content merely with this matching preliminary evidence, early on March 16th and well before putting himself to drafting his report to Judge Fuentes Novella, the commissioner had gone to

Oswaldo Salazar

Cantón Ingenio to interview Don Emilio Barrera, the owner of the pasture Bartolo leased for sowing his crops. There, in the sitting room of the landlord's house, he was received with all due authority. He could not believe his ears when he listened to the deliberate words of Don Emilio, who declared that he had seen the footprints of a person wearing sandals heading in the direction where they had been working. Commissioner Flores did not want to explore this testimony further so as not to bother Don Emilio or offend his dignity. It sufficed to suppose that, on finding out what had occurred on the 15th, the landlord had been to the scene with the explicit intention of looking for some evidence to help in an investigation that would, without doubt, get to the bottom of the case.

After this, Commissioner Flores had returned to his office and prepared to compile a complete reckoning of what had transpired since the moment of the complaint. To demonstrate his efficiency, he informed the judge that hardly had the complainant family left his office than he had sent urgently for officers Óscar Martínez and Julio Gómez Hernández, the cream of the institution he commanded, to order them to capture Pedro Quezada Morales. He made it clear, subtly, that in fastidious fulfilment of his duty he had waited in the police station until his officers had returned with the accused. Moreover, he added, *at the same time (9.15pm) the aforementioned officers also took in the individual Vicente Morataya Pineda, whom I have also taken the liberty of putting at your disposal in the cells, having found him in the company of Pedro Quezada at the moment of the latter's capture within the Sabana Grande farm, the property of José María Godoy within this jurisdiction.* Commissioner Flores' dispatch was concise on this point, and was limited to stating that it was believed Morataya Pineda was guilty of the same crime *since this precinct*, he wrote, *has knowledge that according to the relatives themselves there was enmity with the deceased over family matters.*

Finally, the police report ended on a humorous note that delighted Judge Fuentes Novella and Secretary Alcántara. The honest commissioner put on the record that he had sent for the aforementioned dog to be picked up at the house of Quezada Morales but, he said, with all the seriousness the case merited, *it was not possible to*

From the Darkness

get it because it had fled. Notwithstanding this, he clarified, *if you believe it will be of any use to the investigation, I will order once again for it to be found.*

But the dispatch did not arrive alone. Accompanying it was a bundle of pieces of gourd that, according to Commissioner Flores in his closing lines, *there were eight of, and which had been handed over by Mrs Mauricia Hernández Urbina, common-law wife of the deceased, along with another piece that had been sent to the Director of the National Hospital of this town, who had requested it by telephone.*[3]

The dispatch was received by the secretary of the court in the early afternoon. The fundamental elements of a case that had been opened only a day earlier, as a result of Doctor Rodríguez Padilla's concise message, began to fall into place. The judicial investigating team already had the complete story – the family's denunciation, the suspects duly detained in the local prison, the testimony of relatives and people known by the deceased, conclusive evidence that confirmed they were dealing with a deliberate poisoning and, above all, a corpse from the crime. It was only a matter of waiting for what was thrown up by the results of the judicial investigation, the chemical experts at the Faculty of Pharmacology of the University of San Carlos and the forensic report from the autopsy.

The complaint, from her arrival at the police station until the last of the preliminary police questions had finished, had taken up more time than Mauricia had imagined. It was not until the officer helping Commissioner Flores by typing every word they said had finished the last sheet and its carbon copies that Mauricia had dared to ask the time. Ten to nine, the commissioner had himself answered, but what's the hurry? Mauricia had explained anxiously that it was nothing... that she didn't know... and after a moment's silence she had added that ever since she had picked up Bartolo moribund at the pasture she had not regained her peace of mind, that she felt anxious without being able to avoid it, but that she had to be strong, for my children, she had said, I must survive this setback in life only for them. The commissioner had replied something that Mauricia had not even heard because she was thinking only of getting away, of going somewhere where she could calm her nerves.

Oswaldo Salazar

They had left in a hurry, her in front and the children behind, automatically, without asking questions, their eyes fixed firmly on the dark road. The hot, humid summer air had accompanied Mauricia and her two children through the empty streets. They had walked home without saying a word, as if propelled by something they were unable to comprehend.

The 16th of March had dawned sunny and misty, as on a typical summer's day. Doctor Rodríguez Padilla had risen earlier than usual. The previous night he had warned his assistants to arrive at the hospital at least half an hour earlier because he did not want any delays to what had to be done or, even less, to become distracted by other matters. On arriving, he went to his office and a few minutes later he was already walking to the autopsy hall without stopping to attend the sick that he encountered on the way. He opened the door and there was everything as he had left it the night before, intact, cold, waiting.

Mauricia had also risen earlier, after an unsettled night in the company of an empty space, listening to the muffled, repressed sobbing of Rogelia in the next room. Pedro García appeared early while they were having breakfast and they told him in detail everything that had happened the previous night. At the end of Rogelia's account, Mauricia warned Pedro not to show his face at the hospital, to let the immediate family make all the visits, and said he would have an opportunity to accompany them during the wake and burial. He told them he was changing his workplace and was now going to be at the Los Cuchales farm of Don Abraham Gálvez.

When Pedro left, Mauricia hurried her children along in order to leave as soon as possible and do what remained to be done. Before arriving at the hospital, they had to go to the funeral parlour to check if the casket they had ordered the night before was ready. Mauricia mentally calculated that they would arrive at the hospital early, but it did not matter, on the contrary, that way was better for anticipating setbacks.

By nine-thirty Doctor Rodríguez Padilla had already finished sewing Bartolo's empty body with thick stitches, and his assistants were busy putting the various organs into individual receptacles in

From the Darkness

order to send them to the Faculty of Pharmacology. He walked to a corner of the room where he washed his hands, removed his lab coat and mask and went directly to his office to write the report. Now he was certain of the diagnosis he had made the previous day when examining Bartolo in his house.

As he was leaving, he ran into the family. Seeing their serious, watchful, expressions made him nervous about having in his hands such a delicate case that would surely evolve, if it had not already, into a criminal scandal in the newspapers. He approached Mauricia and told her that, yes, he had found abundant evidence of a massive poisoning, that he was very sorry her companion had to die in this way, and please excuse him because he had to write up his report for the justice of the peace as soon as possible. As he was going, he added that they should be patient, in a while they could take the body and all that remained to do was wash and dress it. He walked alone through the corridor to his office, and when he entered and saw his small typewriter at the centre of the desk, realised he would be writing a report that in the near future would be of capital importance in judicial proceedings. So be it, he said, it has to be that way, and my role in all of this consists of no more than compiling a report comprising all the information derived from my professional labours. He sat down and began to type:

Amatitlán, March 16th 1939
Mr Justice of the Peace
For your attention.

Under legal oath, allow me to inform you that Bartolo García, who was admitted yesterday at eleven o'clock in the morning, died at four twenty pm as the result of acute intoxication, which was verified in the autopsy carried out on the cadaver today.

Yours respectfully, your humble servant

R. Rodríguez Padilla
Head Doctor

The letter was handed in to the justice of the peace at two in the afternoon. Secretary J. Alcántara signed a copy of a receipt for the hospital messenger and ran to the office of Judge Fuentes Novella to show him what had just arrived. He knocked on the door and, without waiting for a reply, pushed it open discreetly, putting his head round it and asking permission to enter.

"Come in, don't worry," the judge said. "I hope you're bringing me what we've been waiting for since yesterday."

"Yes, it's the report from the hospital."

"About time! Even the police commissioner's came before it," he added, getting up from his chair behind the desk. "Let's see," he said as he opened the envelope and began to read avidly, "just what we need, confirmation of what the commissioner told us in his report. But it's very short," he said pensively. After a pause, he added: "I want you to get in touch with the doctor and ask him when the expert opinion of the Faculty of Pharmacology is going to be ready and, above all, what does he expect to find out from it. That is, now we know for certain the man was poisoned, but we don't know anything about the type of poison the killer used. I don't know if what the chemists are going to do can give us this type of information. It's of vital importance for continuing with the investigation and not committing the sin of haste or an injustice against those already detained."

"But why so much fuss if it's not up to us to investigate?" asked Alcántara. "This is something for the police and the criminal court we have to send the case on to."

"Don't be lazy, Jorge," the judge advised him, with a paternal air, "you can't imagine what a case like this can do for our careers in the judiciary."

"Yes, I understand, but ..."

"Let me finish," he continued, and put a hand on his shoulder, "within a few months remember what I'm going to tell you – this case is going to be famous. If you read the newspapers with any regularity you'll see I'm not fibbing. The commonplace suicides or machete killings in villages and on country lanes hidden away in the mountains are daily incidents, but a poisoning doesn't happen

From the Darkness

every day, and in a small town like Amatitlán, so close to the capital, it's even rarer. So the more complete the report we send to the court of first instance, the better. Listen well."

"You know everything – right, my learned friend?" the assistant commented with a cheeky smile.

"Thing is, I've been in this job quite a while and I've seen a few scary things along the way, things it's best not to mention."

"Like what?"

"I'm not telling you. Remember, walls have ears and whatever is said here is heard over there, and when the time comes no-one knows anything and everyone acts dumb. But believe me, this case is going to be something to talk about, and it's better if we get a grip on it from the start."

"Don't worry, I'll put everything into it. In fact, if you don't have anything else for me to do at the moment, I'll get to work straight away. I can find the doctor at the hospital, and then I'll drop into the police station to see what they can tell me about the men they've detained."

"Don't rush. Just get on with the first, and I'll go and have a chat with Commissioner Flores personally."

Secretary Jorge Alcántara went back to work and, as soon as he could, escaped to the hospital to comply with his boss's instructions. Meanwhile, the justice of the peace and municipal intendant, knowing that in a few hours he would have to go and identify the body, dealt with his most urgent business. He was confident that the police station and its senior officers were more accessible at night-time than during the working day. He would eat with his family as usual, wait while the streets emptied little by little and, at about seven, seven-thirty, amble without hurrying over to the police station.

When he was about to leave, he called out to his wife as she followed her nightly routine that he had to go to the police, nothing out of the ordinary, a work thing, and I am going to return as soon as possible, but I don't want you to wait up for me because I may be late. The wife left the bedroom to see him and ask him to take care, saying she would not sleep until he returned. He picked up his bag, walked to the door and went out into the cool street with its locked houses under a deep blue sky in which the stars were just becoming visible. He walked slowly, like someone from the capital who never ceases to be surprised at the gentle pace of provincial life and is determined to enjoy it as much as he can. When he turned the last corner, he made out, about a hundred metres away, the police station with its door on the corner and slender columns like guardians. For a moment he felt that if he went in there he would never come out, he would not be able to find the exit and they would all laugh at him as they watched his useless efforts. He then thought this was ridiculous, he was very capable of dominating the situation, and he told himself there was no reason to be scared if, at the end of the day, it was not the first time he had visited such a place and it would not be the last.

Like Mauricia, the judge found the door half open, as if inviting him to enter, pushed it and walked carefully along the diagonal corridor with its high arches, looking around and calling in a broken, timid voice to anyone who could hear. Suddenly, from the right-hand side, someone answered in a clear and decisive tone.

"Good evening. How can I help you?"

The judge, who had by now almost reached the inner patio, spun round without responding. He was startled. His open eyes and taut, defensive expression revealed his shock.

"I'm sorry, your honour, I hadn't recognised you," said the man, who turned out to be a police officer on night duty.

"Good evening," said the judge, now more confident. "Excuse me for coming here at this hour, but I need to speak with Commissioner Flores. I thought this would be the best time to speak to him without anyone interrupting us."

"Please don't worry," replied the police officer, "forgive me."

He paused for a few seconds then continued:

"But please take a seat. I'll call the chief right now."

He left through a high, wooden door that separated the public area from the private offices.

Judge Fuentes Novella felt cold in that solitary refuge of thick walls and high vaults, a space for echoes and, very often, disoriented doves that made their way in by mistake and then broke their

From the Darkness

wings and harmed themselves trying to find a way out. Far off could be heard the metallic sound of iron doors being shut, like whips lashing the night. And he thought about the people confined behind these doors. Those cells famous for their invulnerability would be so dark, so lonely and cold.

Commissioner Flores' arrival was preceded by a uniform series of steps that resonated ever louder as they approached. The door opened and immediately the commissioner appeared with a decisive air, smiling with the satisfaction of one who is master in his own territory.

"Welcome!" he said, "and to what do I owe the great honour that Mr Justice of the Peace again bestows on me by deigning to come here personally to the humble dominion of a guardian of law and order?"

The judge stood up and, without reacting to the tone of vulgar irony that he perceived in the commissioner's words, extended his hand in the most casual manner.

The commissioner did the same and asked him to, please, follow him to his office, this was not the place to hold a meeting with such an important official of General Ubico, the president.

Mechanically, hating himself for not knowing what to say in critical moments, the judge followed the commissioner through the narrowest and lowest of the passageways until they reached the small office replete with old furniture and even older, disordered, papers.

Opening his arms and signalling for the judge to sit down in a rather dirty armchair, the commissioner said: "Please sit down."

"Thank you," said the judge, at last. "Forgive my impertinence for coming at this hour to deal with a delicate matter."

"Think nothing of it! I imagine you're referring to the case of Bartolo García, the man who was poisoned. Did you read the dispatch I sent you in detail?"

"Yes, it was very illustrative, very complete."

"In fact, I had to hurry an interrogation with the family in order to be able to send you a coherent account with the fewest gaps possible. Of course, we're at the start of the investigation. There's still much cloth to cut."

"Yes, but with the urgency befitting this case your report already contains all one needs to know about the basic facts."

"Well," said Commissioner Flores, superfluously, "there are still several loose ends, such as the mutt that got away when we wanted to grab it, and other things that have only been done but not investigated, like the capture of Quezada and Morataya, for example."

"Yes," commented the judge, "you've put a great success on the record there."

"It was what had to be done, given the denunciation in hand. A bitter pill is best swallowed quickly. But experience tells me, believe me, that it's still not time to hail victory."

"What do you mean? Isn't the case resolved?"

"Between you and me," said the commissioner, moving closer to the judge and speaking in a low voice, "I have already undertaken a small interrogation of them. I told them it was routine but you, better than anyone, know that I shouldn't, it's illegal. And if my chief there in the capital or the judge of first instance finds out, I'm done for. I told them I had to do it, that it was routine when people are brought in to this remand centre."

"And what did you find out?"

"We already know, because of the gossip permeating this town, that Quezada was a declared enemy of Bartolo García. But according to the officers I sent, what they least expected was to find him on the very day of the crime, and at that very time, in cahoots with Morataya, another known enemy of García. It was enough for them to haul him in as well, just in case."

"What did they tell you? Because you were waiting for them, right?"

"That's right, here I was, sitting, working, when these two entered with mortified expressions on their faces."

"Did you interrogate them right then?"

"Yes," he said with a smile, "I like to take advantage of the fear they're feeling when they come through that door. But those two were not only scared, they were also indignant, annoyed. That unsettled me, because it's not common, so I paid attention to what

From the Darkness

they had to say and it seems, from where I'm standing, that they have good alibis and, from what they say, that a lot of people can confirm where they were at the time this crime was committed. But the judge who is put in charge of this mess will have to ascertain this for himself."

"It will fall to me to send Guatemala City a complete report on the case."

"For that reason you're not going to tell them what I told you."

The commissioner paused, turned to look at the portrait of General Ubico behind him, and said:

"Don't forget that The Man sees and hears everything, and just as he raises up some, he sinks others."

"Yes, you're right. Everybody's destiny is in his hands."

"You have to behave yourself, attorney. I've seen a number of judges and intendants from the capital, like you, come through here, young, at the start of their careers, ambitious, who detest living in a small town and count the days until they return to Guatemala City to find better opportunities."

"And? Why are you telling me this?"

"I don't know, perhaps because we both have to give it our best shot and tread cautiously through all of this. I would also like a transfer, to become an investigator in the secret police. I could stop picking up idiots at night-time and sending truants to school when I find them in the street. Don't tell me you want to spend your life as a minor judge in Amatitlán and not carve out a career in the judiciary or in politics, becoming, let's say, a deputy or magistrate for who knows where."

"Yes, sure I'd like that, but you can see I don't aspire to much, and it's not because I don't have ambitions, we all do, but because I'm a sceptic. The law faculty is full of middle-class people who think that with their title they're going to conquer the world. I don't believe that, I think that here talent, ability or good behaviour is worth nothing, and what counts is something else – friendships, family, to mention just the ones I know about."

The officer on duty put his head round the door, embarrassed, and said:

"Commissioner, sir, forgive the interruption, but that journalist is looking for you, I always forget his name, the correspondent of *El Imparcial*."

"See, that's all I needed," he said to the judge. "Let him in."

"What is it? What would he want?" the judge asked.

"Don't worry, leave him to me."

Voices could be heard and the door began to open. A thin man in a creased suit entered, hat in hand.

"With your permission. Am I interrupting something?" he said.

"You never interrupt anything, man," said Commissioner Flores through a wide smile, "come on in and sit down."

The man walked towards them, pulled up a chair and sat.

"And what brings you over here, Jorge?" the commissioner asked.

"Nothing important. But please continue. I don't want to cut the thread of your conversation."

"It was nothing. A chat between friends. To tell the truth, we were talking about our jobs."

"When I came in and the guard told me that Judge Fuentes Novella was here, I thought you could be talking about the death of that peasant who was poisoned by his enemies, so they say."

"And how did you find out?" the judge joined in.

"Okay, okay," interrupted the commissioner, "I've not made any announcements so far."

"As you well know, in Amatitlán everyone knows everyone else. I've known since yesterday, and today I gatecrashed the wake. That's where I've come from. And it was seething with rumours. So what's the truth?"

"About what? What do you know?" asked the commissioner, suspicious.

"That poor Bartolo was in agony all day and on the same night Pedro Quezada and Vicente Morataya were captured, accused by Mauricia, his woman."

Commissioner Flores' expression had changed. Now he was serious, thoughtful, and looked squarely at the correspondent of *El Imparcial*. There was a moment of silence. The judge also looked at the commissioner, waiting to see what would happen.

From the Darkness

"Okay," he said, "now that all the interested parties are here, let's make certain things clear, and I don't want you both to say later that I didn't warn you. They didn't lie to you, Jorge. Things are just as you have said. Mauricia appeared here at seven o'clock with the children, she made a full and direct denunciation of Pedro. I immediately detailed Óscar and Julio and, being very diligent, within a matter of a few hours they had brought me not only Pedro but also Vicente, because they were together and everyone knew that the latter really hated Bartolo. Today I went to the scene of the crime to carry out police inquiries and, by the end of the morning, I was sending my complete report to the judge present here."

"Could I see this dispatch, attorney?" asked Jorge, turning to look at the judge.

"Excuse me, your honour," interrupted the commissioner. "I was getting to that and you didn't let me finish," he continued, now addressing Jorge and pointing at him. "What I'm about to say must be understood very clearly. And this goes for both of you. Nothing has happened here... yet. This is a very delicate case. I don't want anyone putting their foot in it. Experience tells me we don't have all the cards in our hand. The accused deny everything and there are still many things to find out."

"And what are you thinking of doing?" Jorge asked.

"We were discussing this when you arrived," said the judge.

"This is the plan," said Commissioner Flores authoritatively, "we're going to send the file to the court of first instance in Guatemala City, and we're going to request that they maintain the maximum discretion possible so as not to interrupt our investigations here in Amatitlán. What this means is that, for now, I don't want you to go round talking about this, much less newspaper stories or statements to journalists who might come down from the capital. Stay in contact with me, you above all," he said to Jorge. "I'll give you the thumbs up when it's convenient. At the moment I want people to think that we're satisfied we captured the guilty parties almost immediately. That's going to make the job easier. If some accomplice is still walking around free, I want him to feel confident and to be careless. Then we'll see what the course of the investigation comes up with."

"Enough said," the judge commented. "Let's each play our part, and let's stay in touch. I'll have to make some journeys to Guatemala City to explain the situation. But I'm sure they'll understand."

"There's one other person involved," said Commissioner Flores. "It's Doctor Rodríguez Padilla. But don't worry about him. He called me on the telephone to request a sample of the gourd containing the poison. I sent him one and took the opportunity to warn him to be discreet, not to talk about this to anybody, not even his wife. I was going to call you," he added, gesturing to the judge with a contemptuous grimace, "but I'm not used to all this nonsense with the telephone."

"Was he in agreement?" asked Jorge.

"Who?" said the commmissioner, distracted for an instant.

"Who do you think? Doctor Rodríguez Padilla."

"What alternative does he have? You know him, always so cooperative."

"Okay," Jorge said, with resignation, "then all I can do is continue to wait for General Serrano Muñoz to come and make his routine inspection. It's going to be next week. I have time to prepare the article."

"Yes," said the commissioner, "take things easy. Use your pen to give a poetic vision of this beautiful town. Did you read the article this man wrote about the blessing of the church?" he asked Judge Fuentes Novella. "It was poetry, best thing I've read in a long time."

"No," the judge replied, "I missed it, what with so much paperwork; but I'd like to read it."

"Don't worry, I'll lend it to you," the commissioner said. "Just let me find it."

He stood up and flicked through the papers on his bookcase. At last he said:

"Here it is! But can I have it back? I'd like to keep it."

"Of course."

From the Darkness

"It's really nothing special," Jorge insisted. "It's only a small report about the religious rites."

They stood up and the commissioner accompanied them to the door.

Back in his house and alone in the kitchen with a cup of coffee, Judge Fuentes Novella took the opportunity, in the calmness of the moment, to read the poetic report by Jorge, the *El Imparcial* correspondent:

BLESSING OF THE CHURCH OF AMATITLÁN ON SUNDAY IN FRONT OF A PASSIONATE GATHERING BY TOWNSFOLK FOR RELIGIOUS ACT

Amatitlán. A festival of bells on a Sunday morning... A tuneful brass band beneath a clear blue sky. The fluttering of pennants on the façade of the temple, where the high bell towers stand like tutelary sentries of the Catholic people, gentle yet brimming with fervour.

The fervent flock gathered in front of the porch of the church where, on an improvised altar, the Virgin of the Rosary was smiling with ineffable sweetness and the glittering fairy lights stood out from ornately decorated branches; where the wide drapes brought great majesty and in their spirals the whisps of incense seemed to elevate the retirement of the souls.

And beneath the infinite dome of the most grandiose of temples – the blue dome of heaven – began the holy sacrament of the Mass. It is not possible to calculate the number in the congregation, but it was totally crowded. A multitude of men, women and children pressed together in front of the improvised altar, where the flowers and the lights sang out the expressions of a people paying homage to their Creator.

The article continued, but at this point Judge Alberto Fuentes interrupted his reading, let the newspaper fall to the table and lost himself in thought looking out through the window at the night.

From the Darkness

IV

On the night of Saturday the 25th of February Mauricia had announced that on the following day she would get up early to attend the ceremony to inaugurate the new church façade. And, as she expected, no-one said a word about it. Bartolo and Félix took advantage of Sunday mornings for jobs they had fallen behind on in the house, and Rogelia was getting ready to go for an amble with Pedro, far from the curious looks and attentive ears of the family.

No sooner had dawn broken, than Mauricia had risen first and prepared breakfast, and by the time the others began to come in she was already leaving. She knew she would be out all morning and, perhaps, for several hours in the afternoon. Before reaching her destination, she had to go to the church, walk among the people, let herself be seen, chat here and there and lose herself in the crowd.

It was a holiday. Father Pius Jesús Pomet had prepared the formal acts months earlier. The whole of Amatitlán had seen the work progress, step by step. At last, the old colonial church would have a new façade. Many from the locality, mainly members of the closed circle of the Brotherhood of the Infant Jesus of Amatitlán, their wives, the inauguration committee, the Crusaders of the Virgin of the Rosary, and all who aspired to be taken into account in the affairs of the parish, participated actively during the last few weeks constructing and adorning the improvised altar on the porch where the Mass of benediction and thanksgiving would be carried out.

Oswaldo Salazar

When Mauricia left at about half past seven half the town were already making their way to the central plaza. The very furthest streets of Cantón Rosario were empty. As they walked along 5th Avenue looking for 7th Street and leaving behind them deserted roads and closed houses, Mauricia remembered the day that Bartolo, ten years earlier, desperate, had been seeking help to cure his son Lencho and no-one could lend a hand because they were all walking in the traditional procession of the Infant Jesus.

The church was wide open. Hundreds of people were busy, diligently undertaking small, ornamental tasks. As she turned the corner of the park, Mauricia could not avoid suddenly seeing the image of the Virgin of the Rosary right at the centre of the porch, her smile welcoming all who arrived. Father Pius was coming and going, bringing everything together, giving orders, arranging things at the last minute, his tunic blowing in the wind – and in a demonic temper. Everything seemed ready, prepared in good time although there was an atmosphere of tension among those placing or replacing vases, arranging tablecloths, scattering pine needles, reassuring themselves that the structure would stand firm. And all were going about in their best dress – well-pinned mantillas, high heels, white shirts and ties old from being put away for so long. To one side, as if not wanting to be a hindrance, could be seen the mayor, judge and his team of pupil lawyers. They were accompanied by Commissioner Flores and Jorge, the correspondent for *El Imparcial* in Amatitlán.

Mauricia positioned herself within the crowd, looking for someone she knew. She soon bumped into some neighbours, relatives of Bartolo, and people she knew from the market, and began to feel uncomfortable because by now those who had noted her presence were giving her looks, and more than a few people would be able to see her at the very moment when she would have to leave. The number of people grew with each passing minute, making it more and more difficult to move because everyone wanted to be as close as possible and to keep their place. Mauricia moved to one side as well as she could and, when she reached a position from where she

From the Darkness

could depart when she wanted to, there was a sudden silence and the rustle of clothing as people stood up. She made an effort to look towards the altar and could distinguish Father Pius at its centre, to one side of the Virgin of the Rosary, raising his hand and saying in a husky and sonorous tone:

"In the name of the Father, of the Son and of the Holy Spirit, Amen."

In a reflex act, Mauricia made the sign of the cross, but immediately hid her hand. She felt guilty, as if she had profaned something sacred and as if such insolence would bring disgrace, irreparable calamities, upon her. Forgive me, little Virgin, she mumbled. And when the Father finished his ritual introit just before the people would sit down, Mauricia looked around and took the chance to leave without being seen.

It was the third time she had taken this route that she now knew like the back of her hand, the third time in search of the same ultimate destiny, asking herself incessantly what was making her do this and why was she taking such a risk. It was only a matter of a few blocks but, as she walked and looked from side to side, she felt as if time had slowed down and the whole world had stopped around her to watch her pass by. She knew in advance that most of the houses were empty because all those who had eyes and ears to scrutinise her were now spectators at the holy sacrament of Mass. But although this thought calmed her down, it did not stop her looking over her shoulder from time to time. With every passing moment Father Pius's sacred, expressive words, full of reproach and eternal wisdom, sounded further away.

Mauricia quickened her pace to put more distance between them, to put herself out of reach of the good news that the Father was announcing; but it was only when she saw her hurried feet stirring her long skirt that she realised she was heading in the opposite direction, the crosscurrent of the path that the faithful flock had followed that morning. She was moving away from the centre, from the altar where everyone was venerating the Queen of the Universe, Tower of Ivory, Morning Star. She, Mauricia, was of her own volition moving ever further away from that ideal of beauty and virtue with a crown of gold and brilliant white cloak, towards the darkness on the fringes, at the extremes, towards the threshold she had already crossed twice.

Instinctively, Mauricia knew that when she arrived she would gradually regain the peace of mind she had lost the moment she had entered the street minutes before, and could not recover for as long as she continued to see picture cards of the Virgin in little improvised altars in the windows, in the porches, decorations on the cornices, studio photographs of processions, of the Infant Jesus of Amatitlán pointing at her with his tiny raised finger and watching her pass by with his sweet and understanding look. Yes, she had to hurry in order to put all this behind her and give herself over to the emotions of her clandestine tryst.

There, on the other side of that closed door that she could already see from the distance, Hilario was waiting for her. The warm breeze blew lightly across her bare face and seemed like a mute presence, the only one in the empty street.

She knocked twice, quickly and without force, as if her hand was whispering in secret the name of the one awaiting her. The door opened almost immediately and Mauricia went in, looking over her shoulder for the last time. It was dark inside. There was a small living room with a single window that opened to the street, and some old, dusty armchairs that looked like they were never used. As her eyes adapted to the darkness, Mauricia remembered in a flash the first time she had crossed the room holding the hand of this man now hiding himself behind the door who was eager to take her in his arms and who, more and more, was revealing his passion, that contained, postponed force.

The door closed and she saw Hilario in front of her, his expression happy, lustful, eyeing her body, and she felt his hands taking hers and bringing her near, to encircle her with his arms.

"You came at last... I couldn't wait to see you!"

For a moment, Mauricia reconstructed in her mind the past weeks, the day she had entered this house for the first time, the letter, her surprise at seeing how Hilario changed when he touched her, the things, the names he called her, the way the

From the Darkness

relationship had changed, how words had been replaced by touch, romance by desire.

"How did it go for you today? Did anyone see you nearby?"

"No-one, everyone is at the church."

"But you took a little longer. I thought you'd had second thoughts."

"No, nothing like that. I had to act stupid and let them see me. After all, anyone can get lost in that crowd."

"Well, what's important is that you came," he said, and embraced her again.

Mauricia sensed his strength, yet his anxiety about whether she would come and about the time that was flying past and would eventually take her away from him leaving him with just a painful memory, with empty hands and spent words. For a moment she feared that the door would not open again, that Hilario, in his madness, would not let her leave, see the light of another day, would keep her there to use her when he needed, wear her out and in so doing make the solitude even greater. She felt that his twitching hands would run across each centimetre of her body forcefully, blindly, without stopping for more than an instant on whatever they recognised.

"Come, let's go inside," he said.

She did not answer. She only saw Hilario's eyes and thought his gaze was no longer the same, that he was changing. She let him take her hand. They left the living room and walked along the corridor to the door of the bedroom where the previous encounters had taken place. Hilario opened it and let her enter. When he shut the door behind him the room was left in near darkness. Then she saw him walking to the window, and a yellow morning light still illuminating the bed, bedside table, the old frames that hung on the decaying and unpainted walls, and the strong, almost threatening figure of Hilario now turning and walking inexorably towards her. Her intuition told her at that moment that there was something unpredictable about him. He would make love to her, that much was certain, but she couldn't know how, with what degree of violence, what he would call her.

Oswaldo Salazar

Hilario reached her without saying a word, his eyes fixed on her body, on the parts that he was discovering little by little as he removed the garments she was wearing one by one: the shawl, the soft blouse of white silk that slid along her shoulders, the hairpin that stopped her black hair falling freely. Mauricia did not move, she let him do what he had dreamed about since the first time they had seen each other. She remembered the moment her husband had undressed her for the first time, against her will, many years ago. He was drunk, she thought, his breath smothered me and I couldn't move my face away from his clumsy kisses. But now it was Hilario kneeling before her and beginning to untie the girdle that held up her long skirt. Mauricia could see the room as if she were alone. Perhaps out of fear of the violence of men, she was distracted momentarily. She saw the bed where she would be, had been, given over to the penetrating impulse of this trembling old man, who desired her as no-one had ever done before. The bedspread was clean, and the pillowcase as well, as if Hilario had just made the bed. Mauricia thought this flattened, ordered surface would soon be a mess, a map of the passion and the yearning of Hilario to be inside her, never to leave, and to cling on to her body.

She lowered her eyes and there he was, his expression mute, looking at her as if for the first time. And she, standing amidst the circle of her skirt, felt the hot hands of Hilario that had just touched her, the coarse hands of a peasant that had to strain to feel the softness of her muscles, the invisible, bristling down covering her skin. Seeing him so defenceless, at her mercy, Mauricia smiled and, from this height, like a goddess favouring a mortal, without taking her eyes off him, lowered her brassiere to let him see her small breasts, the prize for the anguished wait of solitary dreams.

Then Hilario began to raise himself slowly, looking at her as if she was a revelation, placed his hands on her shoulders and, staring at her intently, slid them across her skin until stopping to rub her dark nipples.

"Now I shall touch you," she told him.

Mauricia smiled again and began to remove his clothing. First the shirt, then the belt. She knew well that now came the spoken rites. And this was what she feared most, because she did not know who he would become. But, without having stopped to think about it, she also knew that this game had excited her since the very first time. Now she would have to lie on her back and repeat what he said to her, do what he wanted.

"Who am I?" he asked from the edge of the bed as she sat.

"My daddy."

"And you? A whore! That's what you are!"

In the porch of the church, meanwhile, the Mass had reached the moment of the consecration.

"This is my body, which shall be given up for all men..." said Father Pius amid a silence of lowered heads and intimate prayers.

Mauricia saw Hilario's eyes and was afraid. He was no longer the same. He looked at her with fury, rancour, like an all-powerful father who punishes without pity, whose wishes, and what he will do, are not known.

"Yes, a dirty prostitute," he continued, as he brought his face close until she could feel his breath.

"Hilario..." she said, forgetting the game for a second.

"Shut up! Hilario's not here, he's gone, he went out that door and won't be back for some time."

"Daddy, don't hit me, I'll do whatever you want," she said.

"That's how I like it. Hilario will be pleased if you behave yourself. He left you with your daddy to teach you a little lesson. And we're not going to cheat him, right? The poor man," he added, pushing her on to the bed, "you can't imagine all the things he thinks about you. And he's worried."

Mauricia fell on her back on the bed. She knew she had to remove her underwear, but not the shoes that he liked.

"And he mustn't worry about you," he continued, "because you're beyond redemption. He doesn't know what you..."

Such long lines of people had not been seen for many years. It could be said that the whole town had gone to take communion when the time came. Father Pius could not manage his interminable task by himself, wrapped in his ceremonial attire and perspiring in the morning sun. Two altar boys followed his lead, one by one: "The Body of Christ." "Amen." And another, and yet another.

"Yes, that's it... that's it...!" Hilario said, on his knees, at the edge of the bed and touching the top of Mauricia's legs as she wrapped them around him, as if he was drowning in deep water.

Now she was in control. From now on, he was in her power. She, her flesh, turned into a sea that could not be tamed by his strength, by his old body, moved to its very bones by desire.

"Poor little baby," she said, ruffling his grey thin hair, now level with her lower belly. "Here I am. Eat, my boy, eat me all up. I'm going to feed you."

"Harlot!" he said, looking at her from down there, below. "You always win... Always... But you are not going to tell Hilario... He'll never know... And don't look at me! He could enter at any moment."

Mauricia shut her eyes and abandoned herself to the feeling of him between her legs as they finally closed around his head. It got better and better because she had shown him, she had given it to him to eat with his mouth and had told him how, when, where. Everything. She had made him hungry and given him the food that is never finished. And there she had him once again – quiet, moaning, a prisoner of this loving enclosure, smooth, drinking the waters of the moment, of desperation.

At last, after struggling through that tumult of people for several minutes, Father Pius was able to stand behind the improvised altar, exhausted, and to finish the sacrament.

"Let us pray!" he said. "Now that we have eaten this bread that gives eternal life and relieves our worldly sorrows, we can go in peace."

The crowd did not move from their places. It was now time for the celebration. But first the Father had to say a few allusive words about the significance of that moment. They had gathered to give thanks and also to inaugurate the new façade of the church.

"That," said the Father, making one last effort, "is not the work of one, or two. Only with the help of the Almighty, in the first place, and through our collective effort, could such a moment arrive that will be fixed fast in the memory of each and every one of us."

Mauricia now felt the uncontainable force of her first orgasm. She opened her legs and her body tensed in a graceful arch. Her twitching hands grasped the ruffled sheets while he concentrated his craving on that delicate, timid spot that only revealed itself when Mauricia went into a frenzy. Finally, when she was relaxing, and beginning to open her eyes, she saw that he had got up and was coming to claim all of her.

"I want to enter... You are going to let me, right? I only want to enter... my home ... my home..." he said, speaking both to her and himself.

Mauricia saw him approach and felt the size of his erection before it penetrated her. It was enormous, larger than before.

"Come," she told him with her arms open, "enter wherever you want."

"Do I have to remind you?" asked Father Pius, once again possessed by the fervour of his faith, "Do I have to remind this Catholic people what I have said thousands of times in my homilies? No, I don't think so. But just as in their day all the saints of the Holy Roman, Catholic and Apostolic church believed it, it's never enough for me to keep reminding you, over and over again – without her, and listen to me well, without HER," he said, pointing to the picture of the Virgin in front of him, "none of this would be possible, it is she who takes us by the hand to eternal joy, she who opens the doors of heaven, the eternal resting place."

The priest – Jorge would write that night, his memory still fresh – *offered a moving piece of holy oratory. His words reached to the very depths of the spirit of his emotional flock and, with convincing fluidity, threaded together phrases of piety, purity and love. Because the temple, elevated today through this homage, is truly something meritorious; moreover, it represents the temple of goodness and devotion that the spirit must itself elevate to Heaven; because there, up above, God wants, other than monuments of stone, monuments of charity, justice and kindness.*

Mauricia felt the blind contact that began to penetrate her depths. She was surprised that he did it with care, softly, and that it came out half way along its journey, to return and enter a little bit more. And, once again, rhythmically, opening the way like someone recognising, full of wonder, a place they should never have left.

"I'm entering you... Mauricia... right inside..." he said, his head resting on her breast.

"Here I am," she answered, feeling the intensifying thrust reaching somewhere nobody had ever dared to go. "I'm yours."

"It is for this reason that we are granted refuge in her shelter," the Father continued, now uttering his final chords. "For this reason we must do, say or think nothing without dedicating it to her. Our lives: what more can we give her in homage to her role as mother? A minimum offering is this porch and this façade that today we hand over to her. Simple ornaments to adorn her house, and our love as lost children who always yearn to knock on her door, pleading to be let in."

Now the pushing was no longer soft, it had turned violent, desperate, and he was no longer resting on her breasts. He had raised himself up and Mauricia could see in his expression the effort he was making; but also a growing shade of hatred, of contempt. It was time for pain.

"Hilario," she said, regaining her senses, afraid, "what's happening to you?"

"Hilario?" he asked. "He's not here. He's far away, waiting for me to give you your well-deserved punishment. He can't, but I can."

"Now," said the Father, "for the final act of the blessing and the cutting of the symbolic ribbon, I want to invite his worship the mayor to accompany me on this platform."

There was a general murmur and movement in the front rows where there were benches adorned with white flowers and a carpet of pine needles. A moment later, from among the throng, the figure of the mayor, dressed in blue, could be distinguished. He climbed the altar and received from the hands of the parish priest some scissors with which to cut the ribbon that had been draped just inside the new doorway.

"Yes I can, because I'm your daddy. I watch over you, I'm always spying on you, and look what I find you doing. Always the same. Whore! A thousand times, whore!"

Suddenly Mauricia felt him leave her body and grasp her with a

From the Darkness

strength she had never felt. He lifted her, turned her around and forced her to lie on her stomach. She tried to turn to look when he was separating her legs and lying on top of her. She could feel his hot, agitated breath on her ear. Out of the corner of her eye she could see him sitting up, putting his hand on her back.

The crowd did not miss a detail. All eyes were on the two authorities preparing to cut the ribbon. The Father held it with his hand and the mayor showed the gleaming scissors to the public, opened them and cut the ribbon with one sure snip.

A salvo of fireworks, bangers and rockets – wrote Jorge in the solitude of his home – *greeted the inauguration of the new façade. Musical notes floated in a hymn of very deep piety and the high bell towers scattered the cacophony of their sounds to the winds.*

The pain struck like lightning, without her being able to tell where it came from. Mauricia tried to avoid it, twisting so as not to allow him to do that. But his weight defeated her, it was useless and impossible to try and stop him. Now he penetrated more deeply and the pain increased. And also the indignation. How could he do such a thing, penetrating her there?

The people applauded and cheered the inaugural act. The Father walked the breadth of the façade blessing each nook and cranny, tossing the holy water and repeating to himself Latin formulas that only he understood.

"That's what you deserve. For being a bad girl," he said, as he pushed forcefully and finished inside her without her even daring to complain.

When Father Pius had finished, chords from a marimba struck up on one side of the porch, while two volunteers set off bangers that rose with a whistle and exploded up above, sending noise to the four corners of the town.

Hilario fell exhausted on top of her and slid off her body before lying on his back. Mauricia could barely move, but she made the effort and, as she sat up, without being able to help herself, she began to defecate abundantly on the bed. Then she began to cry quietly, her teeth clenched.

There followed the Te deum – tapped Jorge, inspired. *Thereafter,*

Oswaldo Salazar

the Hail Holy Queen to the patroness of the town, the Holiest One of the Rosary, which was somewhat imposing and serious. The notes of the harmonium and the vibrant voices rose up warmly along with the aroma of the flowers and the perfume of the incense.

"Don't distress yourself," he said, "it's always like that the first time. This time I had to force you, but the next time you're going to enjoy it, you'll see."

The boom of fireworks and the racket of the people who had gone to the religious service could be heard in the sky.

"Listen," said Hilario, "now we have a new façade."

Mauricia could not talk. The pain had still not gone. She thought about the faces she had seen at the church porch before everything had begun. She imagined how her relatives and people she knew had seen her. Scared, anxious, perhaps, surely they had noticed her nervousness. And now no-one would be thinking about her, they would all suppose she was there, wandering about in the crowd, happy, like everyone else, that the church had a new face. Then she looked at Hilario, who was laughing so calmly about the fact that she was ashamed, and she knew she would never be the same, that she would also have a new look, a wider door, and a fuller life.

Cheers and vivas, *bells, fireworks, bangers and rockets* – Jorge concluded his article, highly satisfied and pleased with his reflections – *sealed this solemn act, whilst the sky, infinitely blue, seemed to have been designed to shelter this poem of fervour...*

The last bangers still thundered across the sky of Amatitlán. Curled up into a ball beside Hilario, and smiling at him when the pain allowed, Mauricia imagined that perhaps they were also exploding for her.

That same morning, when the town had not yet returned to normal after the Mass and celebration, Mauricia slipped through the streets on her way back home. She was confused, unable to think or to make a judgement about what she had just been through. What her body told her was clearer. The pain still throbbed like a vague but constant memory that bids goodbye while promising to return.

When he said goodbye, Hilario assured her that if she left at that moment no-one would see her, that the people had only just begun

From the Darkness

to return and she would go unnoticed. Mauricia listened as if in a dream. She left like a robot, with an absent look on her face, almost without noticing the disorder in the streets, the groups of families she passed who filled the roads as well as the pavements, happily, as if peace would reign in their homes and everybody would love each other and there would never be any problems. She heard some greetings and from the corner of her eye saw more than one person she knew pointing to her when they noticed her walking alone. Where could Don Bartolo be? Had poor Mauricia, married to that old man, come alone? she imagined them asking themselves.

Then she remembered Bartolo lying down next to her snoring, stinking, completely oblivious to her insomnia, and the image made her think all at once that she would see his face again as soon as she got home, that, perhaps, uncaring as he was, he would ask how the Mass had been, if it had all gone without a hitch, if she had seen anyone and if she had been pleased. And she would reply, yes, she had arrived early enough and had not wasted her time, the altar was beautiful, arranged well, with the sweet Virgin in the middle. She would add that, yes, she had seen people she knew, but she didn't remember who because the ardour of the encounter – *spiritual*, she would have to clarify, to avoid being misunderstood – had absorbed her completely. Then he would be satisifed and would go back to his routine, to his ignorant silence, without the slightest suspicion about what had happened between those four walls in that dark room where Hilario had already taken her by the hand three times.

Just as he had promised, the memory of it all came back after a few days. And despite her first impression, Mauricia now wanted to go back to see Hilario sooner than she had imagined. She felt that she was his, permeated by his love; she startled herself as she was bringing her hand to her chest to make the sign of the cross when the idea entered her mind that he was the only man to know her both inside and out, front and back; she remembered herself there, next to him, sobbing, feeling like someone else, feeling him still inside, rigid, implacable, and she felt the desire to go back and give herself to him, Hilario Almeda Godoy, aged 55, single, a native of Amatitlán, known by her husband himself, and a long-standing neighbour in the very same Cantón Rosario.

They met three more times in the following weeks. Three times they occupied the whole morning until past midday. The first, Saturday the 4th of March, when the whole of Amatitlán was reading the article about the inauguration of the church's façade in the '*El Imparcial* in the provinces' supplement. The second, Wednesday the 8th, the day that she took the fatal decision; and the third, Monday the 13th, just two days before the deed would be done.

Despite his advanced years, Hilario was still surprised at how rapidly Mauricia adapted to him during those weeks. Now she sought him out and when they were together she gave him her body fearlessly, without reticence – that is, with the naturalness of someone who knows they have discovered something inside and abandons herself to her pleasure beyond the point of no return.

Yet not only the ritual of touch was longer, slower, more detailed, but also the silences, with only sporadic words, after the yearning and craving of wandering mouths and hands.

On the 8th of March, when it was nearly time to part, Hilario did not know how to answer a question posed by Mauricia. He had noticed that she was pensive, her face resting on his chest and her gaze looking beyond, right through the walls to a point in time.

"If Bartolo died and I was left alone, what would happen to us?" she said, without expecting a reply.

Hilario raised her head to look her in the eyes. She looked at him, smiled and continued saying:

"I mean, because my children are growing up and each of us will go on to shape our own lives."

From the Darkness

V

Commissioner Francisco Flores G., supreme chief of the Amatitlán police and a man of recognised authority, awoke in the early hours of Thursday the 16th of March. Without getting up, as he looked absently at the ceiling, he went over in his mind what had happened since Wednesday afternoon. There, in the doorway of his office, was Mauricia, speaking in a low voice to her two children. The images of her face came in fragments, he could hear parts of incoherent phrases: 'Bartolo... the doctor... then he told me that it had been that damned Pedro Quezada ...' He remembered his officers' expressions when he was giving them instructions: I want you to go and arrest... now... bring him to me today... by the throat if necessary... Their faces showed surprise, it must be something serious, unusual for Amatitlán.

It was useless. Impossible to continue sleeping. He sat up in bed and thought about the long day of police business ahead. Pedro Quezada and Vicente Morataya had been in detention since the previous night, awaiting the instructions of Judge Fuentes Novella, who would soon receive his official letter and prepare to take action. The law obliged the judge to initiate the legal process that, in its first phase, was no more than a mere investigation of the facts. This had been done when the judge had learned of the case from the hospital director's opportune tip. The complete investigation into the circumstances in which Quezada and Morataya had been captured promised to be a solid step towards the quick resolution of a case of homicide.

Oswaldo Salazar

Everything seemed to be going smoothly: a corpse from the crime, Bartolo's last words, the inconsolable widow's denunciation and, above all, the enmity between the victim and Pedro Quezada which, according to relatives of the deceased, was public knowledge. But there, sitting on the edge of his bed, Commissioner Flores did not feel satisfied. Everything was fine, except for the absolute denial by the prisoners. The commissioner had had his doubts the very first time he had heard them, as they were coming through the door of his office. He knew these people, especially these old neighbours from Cantón Rosario. They were capable of killing with machetes over a scrap of land or an insignificant intrigue, but experience told the commissioner, almost without room for doubt, when they were telling the truth or not. And that night their faces, their amazement and indignation, had told him clearly that there was something strange, that most probably an injustice was being committed. That said, the judicial machinery had been set in motion, and although the direction things were taking did not please him one bit, he had to respect not only the judge's authority but also the bureaucratic game of which he was such a bitter critic.

Later, by now heading for his office, he felt that time was slipping away. Soon Judge Fuentes Novella would bring him the resolution of the penal court in Guatemala City ordering the prisoners' transfer to the central penitentiary. Then things would really be out of his control. It was now or never. "How did I let time slip by," he said to himself on the way, looking at the ground he was treading but not the people passing him by. "I spent yesterday attending to the family. Moreover, everything happened very late. We hardly had time to go and haul in the two suspects. And their relatives... what was I going to tell them? The usual: to have patience, that if they were innocent everything would become clear; that, of course, I would keep them in mind. I'd known them all my life, hadn't I?"

When he reached the door of the police station, his subalterns were surprised to see him there so early. They looked at him strangely: his frowning expression, lowered eyes, quieter than usual.

From the Darkness

He went to his desk immediately and sat down.

"I want you to bring me the statement of Mauricia and her children," he said, looking at them with wide open eyes. "But today, lad, what the fuck are you waiting for?"

In an instant the folder of sheets on which the statement had been noted down was in his hands. Commissioner Flores knew nearly every detail of the document; but he had asked for it without thinking, perhaps in the hope of finding something hidden away that he had missed, something key that would confirm his suspicions. He read it from top to bottom at least a couple of times. His assistants remained there, nervous, waiting for a reaction that would explain what the chief had on his mind.

"Last night," he began inquisitorially, "did you confine yourselves to bringing in the two prisoners? Didn't you see something you haven't told me about? Look, this is a critical moment. Anything could be of essential importance. Try to remember."

There was a silence. The officers Óscar Martínez and Julio Gómez looked each other in the eyes, perplexed, and then looked back at the commissioner.

"It was dark," said officer Martínez, "it was difficult to notice anything. We just limited ourselves to carrying out the arrest you ordered."

"The only thing that was our own doing," added officer Gómez Hernández, "was to pull in Morataya as well. But we've already explained this to you and you told us it had been a good idea."

"Yes," the commissioner answered. "I'm not referring to that."

"So?" inquired officer Martínez. "Has something happened that we've not found out about?"

"No," said the Commissioner, sitting back in his chair and crossing his hands behind his neck. "It's just that, I don't know... something doesn't smell good about all of this. We haven't made the most of even half of our opportunities."

"All that remains is to hand them over to the judge, and that's as far as we go," said officer Gómez, aware of the limits to his work.

"No, you're wrong," answered the commissioner with an embittered smile that they had rarely seen. "It's our duty to bring together all possible evidence. Doesn't it seem to you that we are putting a lot of faith in what the judicial interrogation will bring to light?"

"What about it?" officer Gómez Hernández asked again, intrigued.

"Yes," the commissioner continued. "You know these interviews by the lawyers are pure nonsense. It's us who have to figure out the way things truly are."

"And have you already thought of something?" officer Martínez asked.

"I'm thinking about this right now," he answered. "But, let's see: if it's certain what those two say, then naturally there has to be evidence of their innocence in their homes. Their capture was quick and opportune. We didn't give them any time to make ready. And although a whole night has now passed, I want you to go without delay to Pedro Quezada's house and look everywhere to see if you can find the insecticide they say was used to kill Bartolo. Or any other poison they may have. Ah, and don't forget that damned dog that got away the other day!"

"Anything else, boss?," officer Martínez finished.

"Don't come back too soon," he answered. "Search, sniff out, ask the neighbours questions. Do the same in Morataya's house. Go to the fields where they work, speak to the labourers. And talk to Barrera about the footprints he said he'd seen. In the meantime, I'm going to have a chat with the accused. We'll have to send them to the capital at any moment."

The officers left to carry out their orders. The commissioner, for his part, gave instructions to the guards. If the families of the prisoners come, tell them to wait, that I'm complying with the routine requirements of the case.

Later that day, the commissioner picked up paper and pencil from his desk and walked through the corridors towards the cells.

Pedro Quezada and Vicente Morataya, as watchful as they were, jumped with fear when they heard the footsteps accompanied by the sounds of keys and bolts opening the way for someone in authority.

"Gentlemen!" said the commissioner with assurance. "How are we feeling? Like shit, I imagine."

From the Darkness

"Good day, commissioner," answered Pedro Quezada, clutching the bars of the cell. "Any news?"

"Nothing," he answered, "all the same, I want you to accompany me on a little trip so that we can talk calmly."

The last door opened with a cold, dry, metallic clang, and the two men left cautiously, fearful.

"Don't be scared," Commissioner Flores added. "We've known you for years, right? I could sit and wait for that little clerk Alcántara, the court secretary, to come, and let him take you to Guatemala City for them to finish trampling all over you. But no. Today I woke up as the good guy, and I want to give you the benefit of the doubt. Let's go, man, let's go and chat for a while, because the judge is coming so we can identify the body."

The three men walked behind a corpulent police officer with a bunch of keys, who opened the room where they were to talk.

"Stay outside on guard," the commissioner ordered him. "Anything that we need, I'll call you. And make sure no-one bothers us."

"As you say, Commissioner," he answered.

The room was small, with a window to the patio that filled it with light. In the centre were a pine table and some chairs.

"Sit down," said the commissioner, smiling. "As you may have realised, this is not a real interrogation. If it was, I wouldn't have you both here together. That's never done. You are interrogated one by one in order to verify... how do you say... ah, yes, the 'consistency' of the stories. But I don't want to screw you. On the contrary."

"We told you a whole bunch of times already," Quezada said, "we're innocent. This is an injustice!"

"Yes, I know that by heart already," the commissioner answered. "But the truth is, you're here because Bartolo's woman says that you'd threatened his life. So what I want to hear is the alibi. Or rather, where you were for the whole day, with whom, doing what. And when you've told me everything in neat order, I want to know if there's anyone who can verify what you have said."

Vicente Morataya, who had not spoken the whole while, turned to look at Pedro Quezada as if to cede to him the role of spokesman. Not a word was uttered, but the message was understood, and very clearly.

"I'm going to start talking for me personally," said Quezada, putting his hand on his chest, "but after that I will talk for both of us. It's not true that I'd threatened Bartolo. I never forgave him for the dirty trick he played on me over the land, but I didn't threaten him, and even less with death. Anyone in the town can corroborate that. But that's one thing, and another very different thing is whether I've really done it."

"What was this thing about the land all about?" asked the commissioner. "This is the right moment to spell that out. I don't want anything based on gossip."

"Don Emilio," answered Quezada, "as you know, is an honest man, a man of his word. He and his brother Jaime had leased me that plot for two years to sow my tomatoes. And then, one fine day, when I arrived at the pasture, there was Bartolo and his wife cutting all the tomatoes I'd sown. In that moment we said strong things to each other. And later, Don Emilio arrived at my house and knocked on the door (something he'd never done before) to tell me that, no, he'd now decided to give that same plot of land to Bartolo. Can you imagine such a dirty trick? They left me hanging in the air. But it's not the landlord's fault. It was Bartolo's fault. I don't know what he said about me, but Don Emilio came to break the deal we'd made."

"And her?" asked the commissioner. "What was her reaction?"

"At first she was scared; but Bartolo was a hard old man and she felt protected when he was around. There she was, hidden behind him. Now that I think back, she didn't say a word. She just listened."

"And what about that? You know that she made the accusation, right?"

"Yeah."

"So? That doesn't exactly square with her being so peaceful when this confrontation took place.

"That's the thing," said Quezada, pensive. "To be honest, when I'd left, I thought about that."

From the Darkness

"Yeah," Morataya joined in. "That little woman is well-known for being bad-tempered, for treating her children badly, for fighting with everybody."

"It's not for me to tell you what you have to do, commissioner," said Quezada, "but you should investigate her. That woman is hiding something."

"Oh yes? Like what? Do you know something I don't?" he asked.

"Well, it's not us," Quezada said, raising his shoulders, shrugging "but there are rumours in the whole town that she's cheating on Bartolo. Haven't you heard?"

"I'm asking the questions," the commissioner replied, indignant. "Let's see. What is the 'whole town' saying?"

"In that house there's a trapped cat," Morataya interjected. "Ever since Pedro, the fiancé of the eldest daughter, Rogelia, began visiting the house, people have been saying a whole lot of things. Get it?"

"No," said the commissioner, shaking his head. "Don't just give me hints. Tell me what you're saying, loud and clear."

"It's obvious," Morataya continued, "Bartolo is an old man for Mauricia, who's nearly the same age as the boyfriend of the daughter who, in turn, is also very young for him."

"You're a very well behaved man, commissioner," said Quezada "but everywhere, the bars, the football ground, on street corners at certain times on certain days, they're saying that when Bartolo goes to sleep, little Pedro is screwing his woman. And if that's what's being said in gentlemen's circles, can you imagine the women?"

"Well, although it may seem incredible to you," said Commissioner Flores, "I've not heard a thing about this."

"Let's assume it's true," said Quezada, concluding, "then it wasn't me who had a motive to kill him. And if we think about it a bit, that's why she said nothing when I found them at the pasture."

"Why?" the commissioner asked.

"Because if I... let's say... if I had gotten so angry, it saved her or her lover having to invent a story."

"Okay, okay," said Commissioner Flores, trying to be realistic, "we're imagining many things and assuming they're true; and that's not exactly the way I like to work. Let's look at the facts. I want you to tell me where you were on the day."

"Me," said Quezada, moving forward, "I was where I always was. Wednesday, a full working day. I went to the fields very early and I was there with my colleagues from six until eleven in the morning, more or less."

"Me too," added Morataya. "We were working at the same farm: Don Chema Godoy's Sabana Grande, and both of us spent the whole morning watering the young coffee plants. I arrived at dawn and was there until eleven. Ask my colleagues Benjamín Peralta and José Rodríguez. They can confirm what I'm saying. My life never changes, every day's the same."

"And why did the officers find you in Pedro's house?"

"Okay," he answered, "there's no reason why I would lie to you. You know as well that I have my differences with Bartolo. One day his son Félix and some other blokes gave my wife a kicking and beat her real bad. So when I heard about his death, I couldn't resist the temptation to tell Pedro. That's why I went to his house."

"And you?" the commissioner asked, turning to look at Pedro Quezada. "Is that where you found out, or did you know already?"

"I knew already."

"Who told you? How? Why?"

"My wife Ángela," he said confidently. "Poor thing, she was so nervous. I'm sure she thought I'd killed him. But she calmed down because she quickly realised I knew nothing. She knows me very well. She noticed how the news hit me. And it hit me because it's difficult to get used to the idea that a person one's seen as healthy, working, doing the same job as oneself, suddenly stops existing."

There were suddenly three loud, very clear knocks at the door. Pedro Quezada went quiet and they all turned to see what it was about.

"Come in!" said Commissioner Flores in a loud, hoarse voice.

"Excuse me, Commissioner," said the guard who had been left at the door. "I've come to tell you that they've just given me a message that a few minutes ago a committee from the court arrived, and they want to speak with you."

From the Darkness

"Tell them," he said with a frown, "to go to my office and wait, we're coming."

"As you say, Commissioner!" the guard said, fixing his eyes on a point above his chief's head.

Commissioner Flores turned to look at the prisoners without saying anything. For a moment, there was an expectant silence.

"They've come to take you," he said. "From now on you'll be beyond my control. I trust in God that everything you've told me is true; if not you're going to be well screwed."

"Now what?" asked Pedro Quezada.

"I don't know, I imagine they're going to question you; but one never knows. These lawyers always come up with some new nonsense."

The three men eventually left and walked to the commissioner's office. There they met Judge Alberto Fuentes Novella and official Alcántara seated comfortably and chatting as if everything was routine.

"Your honour," the commissioner joked, "you don't show up at this humble department for nothing. There has to be a dead body involved."

The two men laughed while extending their hands. Pedro Quezada and Vicente Morataya could not share the camaraderie of the officials. Rather, that cheerful greeting had seemed to them part of an effort to fulfil their obligations as quickly as possible.

"No, man!" the judge answered. "It's always a pleasure to call in and say hello. But tell me, how are things going? Did you have time to question the suspects?"

"Nothing official. You'll be aware that I've known them for years. We've just chatted like friends. And I only wanted to know what they had to say in their defence. Interrogating them in depth, taking forward the investigation, that's your role. But if we can help you in anything, you know..."

"Thanks," said the judge, slapping the commissioner on the shoulder, "today all we're going to do is identify the corpse or, as they say technically, the body of evidence. Tomorrow we're going to proceed with the transfer of the prisoners to the corresponding penal court in Guatemala City. But, if it's not too inconvenient, it would please me greatly if you accompanied us in carrying out this formality."

"Of course! We're here to serve!" the commissioner answered.

The commissioner, judge and official walked ahead. As they left, the sunlight dazzled them but they still noticed that a small group of onlookers had stopped and was watching, open-mouthed. It was clear that news had spread that the judge had arrived to take the prisoners, and people wanted to watch, wanted to see on their faces what they had never even imagined – that they were killers. The commissioner made a path for them to the vehicle. Pedro Quezada and Vicente Morataya walked the short distance with their eyes locked on the ground amid the dull hissing and murmuring. The doors shut, the motor began to purr and a few seconds later they left in the direction of the hospital.

There, in the doorway, Doctor Raúl Rodríguez Padilla was waiting for them in his capacity, of course, of director of the establishment. Beside him, to assist in the judicial formality, was a young man dressed in white, his hair slicked back and his moustache trimmed.

"Allow me to introduce you," said the doctor, turning to his companion, "to my intern Guillermo García Guillioli."

After the formal greetings, the group moved on to the morgue under the curious eyes of patients and support staff. Until they reached the door, Doctor Rodríguez Padilla had been speaking at ease, moving his hands and using short, confident phrases. However, when he opened the door to the coarse slabs with the spectacle of a body covered with a white sheet on one of them, they continued walking but now in silence and more slowly. The group spread out within the room: the doctor and his assistant approached the body, the commissioner and the judge stayed a few steps back, and Pedro and Vicente were the last. When they had all stopped, the commissioner turned to watch the prisoners and, with a gesture of his head, ordered them to move closer. The junior doctor kept his hand on the hem of the sheet, waiting for the moment when the judge would authorise him to uncover the body. The prisoners

From the Darkness

stopped just a few steps away, downcast. Finally, the judge, half closing his eyes, told the official: please proceed.

Alcántara mentally imagined the final form of the document that he would have to write to the court on return:

It being the 16th of March 1939, and being present as witnesses Messrs Francisco Flores Gálvez, Amatitlán Commissioner of Police; Doctor Raúl Rodríguez Padilla, Director of the Hospital; and the intern Guillermo García G.; Mr Justice of the Peace and Municipal Intendant, Attorney Alberto Fuentes Novella; within the installations of the Amatitlán Hospital, the identification of the cadaver of Mr Bartolo García Morán by the two prisoners Pedro Quezada Morales and Vicente Morataya Pineda proceeded. When asked if he, Pedro Quezada, married, an agricultural worker, from the village of Llano de Ánimas Farm and a neighbour of the Sabana Grande Farm, had known during his lifetime the person on show, he responded yes, that he had, and that they were dealing with Bartolo García and he had known him for years. When asked if he had had any enmity towards him and if he had threatened him with death in the past, he responded categorically no, that they had always had cordial relations and that during his lifetime he had not had any motives for threatening him. For his part, the prisoner Vicente Morataya Pineda, thirty-six years of age, single, farmer, from the village of El Pepinal and a neighbour of the Sabana Grande Farm, said yes, he had known who in life had been Bartolo García Morán, that there had never been any differences between them and that he had never had a motive to kill him.

Pedro Quezada looked at the cadaver only when required to do so. But the rest of the time he kept his eyes fixed on the ground, confining himself to answering the judge's questions. It was not until everything was finished and the tension had relaxed considerably that, little by little, he had turned towards the inert body in front of him. There was that man he had hated so much, whom he had really wanted to see dead when he had found him gathering the tomatoes that it had cost him so much work to grow. But now, faced with this thing that was, in fact, anything but Bartolo, he felt none of the old rancour but, rather, an emptiness inside, a type of involuntary liberation. His eyes ran over that cold, uniform, shiny, waxy paleness that corpses have. And there, amidst this veil of death, was the recently sewn wound of the autopsy. From the lower abdomen to the neck. Its bloodied colour was violent, the stitches brutal, and the wrinkled skin... my God... it was monstruous how they displayed a corpse emptied of its organs. Finally, almost with distress, he dared to look at the face. The mouth was open and the half-shut eyes left a white line visible beneath the eyelids. For an instant, just when they were about to leave, it seemed to Pedro that Bartolo was happy, that he was enjoying an infinite peace far from all the little, petty human complaints, convinced at last that life goes on and that it is better to let yourself be swept away by the force of its flow when death calls.

They said goodbye. Judge Fuentes Novella, in the name of justice, thanked both Doctor Rodríguez Padilla and Commissioner Flores Gálvez for their collaboration. He said goodbye to the prisoners and warned them that the following day, prior to transferring them to the detention centre in the capital, he would have to take complete statements from them at the court.

Commissioner Flores had been distracted during the proceedings. At root he knew that he could have done much more than he had up until now. But in that moment, he resolved to head for the police station with the prisoners. They were lent a carriage to take them to their destination. When he arrived, officers Óscar Martínez and Julio Gómez were waiting at the door of his office with good news. They told him they had searched through everything in the houses of Mauricia Hernández, Pedro Quezada and Vicente Morataya, and had found no trace of poisonous substances; but they also told him that, with a bit of digging here and there, they had a list of possible witnesses for a future opportunity. And the good news was that this time they had been able to capture Pedro Quezada's dog and had brought it with them in case this was necessary. The commissioner wanted to see the dog immediately in order to fulfil the promise

From the Darkness

he had made to send it on when he had managed to get hold of it.

Towards the end of the afternoon, like the colophon to a particularly turbulent day, Commissioner Francisco Flores sat alone in front of the typewriter and wrote:

Amatitlán, 17th of March 1939
Mr Justice of the Peace
For your attention.

Allow me, for your convenience, to send you the dog that is the property of Pedro Quezada Morales, to which I referred in my dispatch No. 273 of yesterday, which is a blackish, skinny, yellow-bellied bloodhound of regular size.

Respectfully yours, your humble servant,

Francisco Flores G.
Commissioner of the National Police

He dated the note the following day to save work in the morning. He knew that, very early, the judge and his assistants would be going ahead with the judicial interrogation and he did not want to miss it for anything in the world.

On Friday morning, using the excuse of taking the note and the dog in person, the commissioner arrived at the courthouse and asked for permission to stay and listen to the prisoners' declarations. Judge Fuentes Novella had no problem allowing him to do so. Moreover, he thanked him for his initiative because he could help take note of all the details and loose ends in the story.

Paper in hand, with Secretary Alcántara the commissioner noted down everything he considered important. At first sight, it seemed to him that there were no contradictions between what he had just heard and what, informally, they had told him in the police station the day before. Now all that was missing was to corroborate the alibis, look at the consistency of the stories, garner the views of the witnesses who had been mentioned. But for this it was necessary to wait several days for the penal judge in Guatemala City to give the order.

The interrogation ended more quickly than he had imagined. By mid-morning the prisoners had returned to the jail and the judge warned the commissioner to be ready because, at any moment, he would have to take them to the capital together with the documentation and pieces of gourd they were keeping as evidence.

On the return journey, the prisoners did not open their mouths. The commissioner, for his part, had to restrain himself from confessing to them that the more he learned the more he believed them innocent. But mentally he grew even more determined to leave no stone unturned in order to ensure that an injustice was not committed.

It went past noon and into the early hours of the afternoon. The commissioner sat alone in his office, expecting the judicial dispatch. Outside, the car that would take the prisoners to the capital was waiting. At four there was a knock on the door:

"By your leave, Commissioner!"

"Come in."

"They have sent you this document from the courthouse," said the guard .

"Thanks, you can go," he answered.

When he was alone, he put on his desk a sealed envelope addressed to the Criminal Judge of Guatemala City, a folder with judicial documents and a see-through bag, duly closed and labelled, in which could be seen the pieces of gourd that the director of the hospital had provided. He unfolded the note that instructed him to proceed in accordance with the provisions foreseen in law, and read:

Guatemala City, 17th of March, 1939

Commissioner Francisco Flores Gálvez
National Police, Amatitlán division
For your attention.

I, the undersigned Justice of the Peace and Municipal Intendant,

From the Darkness

Alberto Fuentes Novella, officially hand over to you the physical evidence that, to date, it has been possible to gather in the case of the death of Mr Bartolo García Morán, as well as the 18 sheets of documentation accumulated by this judicial department and a letter addressed to the Fourth Judge of First Instance of Guatemala City, requesting you to ensure that all the above reach the aforementioned Judge together with the prisoners Pedro Quezada Morales and Vicente Morataya Pineda as soon as possible. Without further ado, respectfully yours, your humble servant:

Attorney Alberto Fuentes Novella
Justice of the Peace

Several days passed. On Tuesday the 21st of March, in the afternoon, the commissioner received a call from Judge Fuentes Novella.
"Commissioner?" he said. "It's Attorney Fuentes."
"How are you?" he answered. "Any news?"
"What we were waiting for has arrived at last," said the judge with relief. "I have just received the order from the Fourth Judge to carry out a thorough inspection of the houses of Pedro, Vicente and Mauricia. But that's not what's most interesting. We already know we're not going to find anything. The good thing is that he ordered us to investigate Emilio Barrera, Benjamín Peralta Osorio, José Rodríguez Peralta and Ángela Catalán, Pedro Quezada's wife. He also wants us to investigate Bartolo's relatives: the wife, the children, the sister, Bartola Santana, and Pedro García, Rogelia's boyfriend."
"So tell me how you want to deal with them."
"I don't know what you think," the judge explained, "but in my opinion it's better to start with the witnesses and leave the family till last."
"Yes," the commissioner, answered, "the family members will only limit themselves to repeating what they said in their original denunciation. The witnesses, by contrast, can tell us something new."
"Agreed," concluded Judge Fuentes Novella. "I'll send the subpoe-

nas and so we'll start tomorrow in the morning if possible. How does that seem?"

"Of course. All I ask is that you allow me to be present at these interrogations."

"That goes without saying. You're the only one who can lend a hand in this. What we're looking for, according to the Fourth Judge's dispatch, is to establish through the testimonies if what the prisoners have said is true."

"I don't know if you're aware of this," the commissioner commented, "but I'm now giving this special attention and I can tell you the whole town is seething with rumours. Something will come out of this, I'm sure of it."

"Yes, I was aware of that," said the judge. "In my own house they don't talk about anything else. One simply doesn't know what to believe now. Nor in whom. Regardless of how much experience you have in these controversies, there are always surprises that leave you open-mouthed. Let's get to work."

"We'll begin first thing," the commissioner said, standing up.

"Done. We'll be waiting for you."

On Wednesday the 22nd of March, just a week after Bartolo's death, the day dawned radiantly, with a dry, static heat. The entire town knew that on that morning the witnesses would be questioned. Only a few minutes after the courthouse opened, those required to make judicial statements began appearing: the work colleagues, Pedro's wife, Don Emilio Barrera.

Out of consideration for her feminine condition, Judge Fuentes Novella decided that the first to appear would be Mrs Ángela Catalán de Quezada, 33 years old, married, a native and resident of Amatitlán, of domestic occupation, and with her home in the Cantón Ingenio district of the jurisdiction.

For obvious reasons, the judge avoided asking if she knew the prisoner Pedro Quezada; but, taking into account the accusatory declarations against him, proceeded immediately to ask her if it was true that, on falling ill, she had used 'sublimate' to treat sores on her legs. As is well-known, explained the judge, 'sublimate', which

From the Darkness

has significant curative properties if applied externally, can be a potent poison if ingested orally. In the face of this erudite question, the witness said yes, that it was true she had been sick, but that this had been nearly three years ago. And she had never had sores on her legs, from which it could be deduced that she had never had 'sublimate' in her house, a circumstance that the envoys of Commissioner Flores here present, she said, had corroborated the day they arrived to search my home.

When the judge was satisfied with the information given by the witness, he proceeded to interrogate the minor José Rodríguez Peralta, aged 13, an agricultural work assistant at the Sabana Grande farm, from that neighbourhood and still living under his father's roof.

In a paternalistic manner, with a half smile on his face, Judge Fuentes Novella moved his chair closer to the witness and made him mindful of the seriousness of the act. Are you aware, he said, what this means? Did your parents explain to you what this procedure involves? You don't have to be scared, we only want to ask you some questions. That means you mustn't lie to us, you must tell us the truth. Is that clear?

The witness sat in silence. The judge returned his chair to its place, took his papers and continued:

"Tell me if you know Messrs Pedro Quezada Morales and Vicente Morataya Pineda."

"Yes, I know them."

"Tell me how you know them."

"They work in the Sabana Grande farm of Don Mario Godoy, where I help with whatever work is offered me."

"Tell me if on Wednesday the fifteenth of the current month the prisoners turned up for work and at what time."

"Yes, they arrived as they always did, at six in the morning, the time all of us go in."

"Tell me if any of them, for whatever reason, was absent during the morning."

"No. I remember that both were there continuously from six until eleven in the morning and that they didn't budge from the place."

Oswaldo Salazar

Judge Fuentes Novella stood up and walked towards José. "That's it, you can go, thanks for coming."

Only two witnesses remained: Benjamín and Don Emilio. Both were key. The judge paused for a breather. If these people don't say anything, he thought, things are going to get very ugly for Pedro and Vicente. Accustomed to basing what he did on the facts, Judge Fuentes had the same fears and hopes as Commissioner Flores. However, in order not to hinder the investigation both had kept their suspicions secret. For a moment, the judge looked at the commissioner seated in the corner ordering his notes, and thought that everything now depended on him, upon the way he steered the questions. The thread that justice hangs from is that thin, he thought; but one was not taught that at law school.

"Please," Alcántara said to the officer, "bring the next witness forward."

This was Benjamín Peralta Osorio, 42 years old, a farmer, who lived with his partner, resident of Amatitlán, with a home in Cantón Ingenio and at that time labouring on the Sabana Grande farm in that jurisdiction.

With his hat on his legs and making an effort to speak clearly and loudly, the witness denied having known the deceased and any member of his family; but, in the following statement, affirmed that, yes, he knew Pedro Quezada and Vicente Morataya because they had all worked together for some time on Don Godoy's farm irrigating the coffee plantation. Look, he explained to the judge, they don't always make us do the same thing, so I can't tell you that I do just one thing. Same with them, the accused. That day, as I've already told you, they put us to irrigating the nursery on the coffee plantation. And were they there all morning? interrupted the judge, steering the declaration back to the main issue. To which the witness responded without hesitating that he could confirm, having seen them there with his own eyes, that neither left work between six and eleven in the morning. I'll swear to you whatever you want, he finished. The judge looked at him for an instant without repeating the question. He knew this was the moment of truth. Then he launched into asking if he had heard any rumours related to the

From the Darkness

death of Bartolo García Morán and, if so, what they were about. To which the witness replied yes, everyone was going around chattering about it in their homes, the fields, the shops, and all agreed on the same point, that he couldn't understand how they had called them in to make declarations but not the members of the family, since it was public knowledge that those in the household, mainly the wife, who was well-known for being an extremely bad-tempered person, were suspected. The judge, now indignant, replied immediately that this was the exclusive prerogative of the judge of first instance of Guatemala City and they were only carrying out orders and accumulating evidence to enrich this process.

At this point, the interrogation was interrupted at the judge's express wishes. The witness, repeatedly saying sorry, left the room. Enthused by the results he had just begun to harvest, Judge Fuentes then brought in his star witness: Don Emilio Barrera, 54 years of age, married, a farmer, native of Amatitlán, of that neighbourhood.

The judge had decided to be more formal with this man, to impose his authority as a public official. Consequently, and despite the little things that came out during his declaration, a certain distance was kept between judge and declarant. It was better that way, thought the judge, as he began a programmed series of questions.

JUDGE: Tell me if you knew both the deceased, Bartolo García Morán, and those accused of his death, Pedro Quezada and Vicente Morataya.

WITNESS: Yes, I had known Bartolo for many years. In the same way, the accused.

JUDGE: Tell me if it is true that the prisoner Pedro Quezada Morales owed you rental for a plot of land that he had used for years, to grow tomatoes.

WITNESS: Yes, it's true; but let me explain some details that make your question inexact. May I?

JUDGE: Speak.

WITNESS: In reality – he began recounting – *he did not owe the money to me. He owed it to my brother Jaime, Jaime Barrera, whom*

Oswaldo Salazar

God now has in his bosom. And in relation to that, I have something to tell you that's going to interest you.

JUDGE: Continue.

WITNESS: It turns out – he continued saying *– that my brother never went to charge him at his house, or even when he was in the pasture working on his crops. He sent Bartolo whom he sometimes asked to be a collector. This is normal, your honour, because it gets results. Imagine sending the person most interested in renting that same piece of land to collect the debt. He's going to do it well, right?*

JUDGE: Tell me if you knew that Bartolo García was interested in this plot being rented to him.

WITNESS: Yes, of course. My brother told me many times. He'd promised Bartolo that if he was successful in collecting the debt, he'd be the next person to lease that piece of land.

JUDGE: Tell me if you had knowledge of any enmity between the deceased and the prisoner Pedro Quezada.

WITNESS: Not that anyone has mentioned this to me – he said *– no. I'd be lying if I said yes. The only thing I had evidence of is what I've just told you. And if you ask me, I'd tell you that this was a sufficient motive for them to stop talking and to avoid each other. At my age, I've seen many things. And that's one of the most common down on the farms.*

JUDGE: Tell me if you have heard any rumour related to the case of the death of Bartolo García.

WITNESS: Yes, no more or less than what the whole of Amatitlán has been going round saying, that the suspect should be the wife, that Mauricia.

JUDGE: Can you expand on this?

WITNESS: Of course. What people are saying is that shortly before dying her husband had hit her. And it wasn't the first time, so they say. That, together with the fact that it's said she has a very bad temperament, is what now has the whole town saying it was her, that poor Pedro is carrying the can but has nothing to do with it.

There in the corner all the while, not saying a word, was Commissioner Flores. He noted down everything he could and,

From the Darkness

afterwards, compared his notes with those taken down by Secretary Alcántara. Amidst the tumult of witnesses, members of the family, onlookers and police officers, he had almost gone unnoticed. Judge Fuentes thanked him for attending and made him promise that they would meet up soon. He left by the door of the courthouse, from where the people had still not dispersed. He walked slowly, in the shadows of the early afternoon, chewing the subject over, worried about how he could find an explanation that made sense of what, for now, was nothing more than suspicion, gossip and a mountain of loose ends.

The following day, Thursday the 23rd, the interrogation of the family would be carried out. Nothing significant was expected from this procedure. Only a tedious repetition of the stories that had sparked the whole commotion in the first place. Nevertheless, Commissioner Flores was not going to lose this unrivalled opportunity to hunt for something: the lost piece of data, the discordant note, the significant omission that would expose the true guilty one, or ones.

Again, first thing in the morning, the judge began the series of interrogations. With a knack for what he was doing and without prompting, he decided that first would be the children and so, suddenly, he separated them from their mother, who had to wait outside.

Rogelia, obviously warned exhaustively, did not vary by one word her statement of a week before. But when it was the turn of Félix, the youngest of the declarants, Judge Fuentes was astute enough to inquire about the type of relationship his parents had.

"Tell me if your parents maintained a good relationship," he asked, getting straight to the point.

"Yes," he answered hesitantly, "well, for a long time they've lived peacefully."

"Does that mean," the judge cross-examined him, "that there was a time when they didn't get on?"

"Yes," he said, lowering his eyes as he explained, "that was two years ago. At that time they had many rows because my Ma is kind of bad-tempered."

Oswaldo Salazar

The commissioner raised his eyes from his papers when he heard these words. At last he had heard something that made sense of some of the things he had been getting wind of over the last few days. The judge had also been surprised by the response and, for a moment, his eyes met those of the commissioner in the complicity of comprehension.

In a reflex action, the judge decided to interrupt Félix's interrogation at this point. The commissioner agreed, because it was obvious that the witness had regretted saying his parents did not get on, albeit in the past. This confirmed, moreover, that he had been robustly warned and threatened about keeping only to the facts declared on the day of his father's death.

When it came to the turn of Pedro García Gesenäuer, Rogelia's betrothed, the commissioner leafed through the file that Secretary Alcántara had entrusted to him. In it was recorded, over and above generalities, certain important details that, to Commissioner Flores, appeared curious, worthy of being investigated further. For example, some years earlier, "for reasons of force majeure", said the declaration, the witness Pedro García had had to abandon Amatitlán to go and work on the coast in search of better opportunities. His judicial statement had no relevance whatsoever and, as a result, the commissioner had noted down hardly anything that he did not already know or suspect. He merely heard what Pedro Quezada had told him a week before from his own mouth: that the young man had been visiting Rogelia's house for three years and that, yes, naturally, he had said, he came every day to talk to her, and that the parents now considered him another member of the family.

Pedro appeared very sure of himself, prompt in his replies and even indignant about the tragedy that had shattered the happiness of the García Hernández family. The commissioner looked at him suspiciously from the other end of the room. His expression did not change when those remaining came in: the very same Mauricia, and Bartola Santana.

The following days, from the 24th of March to the 2nd of April, were particularly barren for the judicial investigation. Searches of

From the Darkness

the homes of Pedro Quezada, Mauricia Hernández and Vicente Morataya, as well as the detailed interrogations of Federico Castellanos de León and Juana and María Peralta, all turned up nothing. Commissioner Flores felt the case slipping out of his hands. But on the 3rd of April, there was some relief when he found out, through Judge Fuentes Novella, that the Fourth Judge of First Instance had granted Vicente Morataya Pineda conditional release for lack of evidence against him, there being no point in continuing to detain him.

A relief, yes, but there remained Pedro Quezada. That very same day, in the judge's office, the commissioner found himself holding the technical report provided by Julio Valladares M. Skipping, director of the forensic chemistry laboratory at the Faculty of Pharmacology and Natural Sciences. Skirting over the incomprehensible technical details, he read at the end of it that in Bartolo García's viscera had been found sufficient evidence of the remains of arsenic mixed with the chemical components of insecticide used against countryside pests.

From the Darkness

VI

Holy Week promised to be especially rich in displays of religious fervour. The inauguration of the façade of the church had brought together two particularly significant events: the recent coronation of Cardinal Eugenio Pacelli as Pope Pius XII, number 262 in direct succession from Saint Peter himself, no less; and also the recent selection of Monsignor Mariano Rossell y Arellano as metropolitan archbishop. All occasions for joy for Guatemala's Catholic flock, said the Fathers in their Sunday services.

The newspaper headlines and leading articles debated the church's good news, the achievements of General Ubico's government and, of course, reporting from the clamour of the European war.

GERMANY WILL NOT WAIT TO BE COMPLETELY SURROUNDED, ITALIAN MILITARY OCCUPATION OF ALBANIA IMMINENT

GOVERNMENT OF THE REPUBLIC HIGHLIGHTS ANOTHER MAJOR FINANCIAL TRIUMPH: KREUGER AND TOLL PUBLIC LOAN PAID

On Tuesday the 4th of April, at about midday, while Commissioner Flores struggled with his papers looking through the statements for a weak point, a revealing mistake, a veiled confession, the correspondent Jorge appeared at his office with *El Imparcial* under his arm.

"May I?" he asked from the doorway.

"Come in," said the commissioner, a little surprised. "What brings you here?"

"I was passing by and decided to come in and ask if there was anything new in the García Morán case."

"I'd like nothing more than for there to be something new!" said the commissioner with a certain bitterness. "But no, nothing. Only the same, what we all know about. And what about you, wandering around asking everyone questions, have you learned anything?"

"Nothing. Same as you," he answered. "In fact, I've come from the court and there they don't know a thing."

"Really? Tell me, did you speak to the judge?"

"Yes, for a moment. But I didn't want to be an inconvenience. All the lawyers there were talking about a report that appeared today. I didn't know what they were going on about until I read the story carefully."

"And what's it about?," asked the commissioner, ever attentive to gossip, above all if it involved the town's attorneys.

"Take a look for yourself," answered Jorge, showing him the newspaper. "Look for 'Personal and Social'."

"This?" he asked, putting his finger on the portrait of a skinny, bald man with an anxious expression and trimmed moustache.

"Yes. That's the story."

The commissioner was lost in thought for a few minutes while he read:

This morning deep sorrow hung over the house of the esteemed Asturias Rosales family in Avenida Central, number 106 after the tender passing of Attorney at law Ernesto Asturias.

Attorney Asturias had been suffering grave afflictions to his health and had had to submit to various medical treatments and, in recent days, to be confined to his bed, where science and the devoted attention of his loved ones coincided to provide him with the most diligent care.

From the Darkness

The news has brought together in this house of mourning a gathering of numerous friends, all of whom stand in sincerity by the family with its heavy burden, thereby multiplying the displays of condolence shown by city society, to which El Imparcial extends its own.

The learned Ernesto Asturias was a distinguished element of Guatemalan life, even if during the last few years of his sickness, and as a result of his singular modesty, he had to be secluded in his home.

A member of that generation of lawyers from the end of the last century, he had attended primary and secondary school at the College of Infants, when the said establishment was the best of its kind and shaped characters under the direction of the unforgettable Father Rubio y Piloña, its rector.

He received his honours degree in the year 1888, in what was then called the Central Faculty of Law, in whose lecture halls he was an object of admiration and appreciation among his colleagues and teachers.

He proceeded to occupy high positions in the judicial profession: Judge of First Instance of Quetzaltenango, Judge of First Instance of this City, Magistrate in the Court of Appeal in Quetzaltenango, Military Judge Advocate in the Field, Judge of First Instance in Salamá and El Progreso, Military Judge Advocate General, and Deputy Magistrate of the Court Martial.

Apart from this, he undertook municipal roles on various occasions and was, for several years, professor in the Faculty of Juridical and Social Sciences. In all the positions that he occupied he committed all his effort, honour and willingness to work, earning the confidence and gratitude of his superiors as well as the appreciation and affection of the public.

And in his personal life, he cultivated a home adorned by the highest virtues of his dignified wife Doña María Rosales de Asturias and extolled by their children, Attorney Miguel Ángel Asturias and Mr Marco Antonio Asturias. The figure of Attorney Ernesto Asturias was popular in the districts of Candelaria and Parroquia, always at the door of his house, wearing a modest cap, waiting to give free counsel to a client, to act in his defence or even to help financially. Perhaps it will be this phase of his life – lawyer for the poor, spontaneous and generous – that will be the last reflected in his expression, full of soft seriousness, of calm sombreness, when he wearily closed his eyes.

At ten o'clock tomorrow there will be the interment of his remains in the General Cemetery. Peace be over the tomb of this citizen and friend, and may there be resignation in the hearts of his relatives, to whom we reiterate our heartfelt condolences, and in particular to his widow, Doña María de Asturias, to our beloved colleague and man of letters, Miguel Ángel Asturias, and to Marco Antonio Asturias, the host at the Casa del Niño orphanage in Barrio Candelaria.

"So?" asked the commissioner. "Why so much fuss about that old man?"

"Well, according to what they said there in the courthouse, it seems he was a very respected lawyer, with a long career. But what caught my attention was that he was the father of Miguel Ángel, the poet who worked as a correspondent in France for years and now lives here with his family."

"Is that the one who talks on the radio? He has that programme... what's it called?"

"*The Daily on the Air*," clarified Jorge. "Yes. That's him."

"Would you look at that. This shyster lawyer ended up as a journalist."

"He's also a writer," said Jorge, becoming annoyed at the commissioner's pejorative tone.

"Known in his own house and thereabouts. Well, fine, but that's not what interests me. What about the García Morán case?" he asked. "Did they say anything?"

"Nothing. You know what these people are like: once they've sent the case to another 'instance', as they say, they wash their hands of it and don't want to know anything about the matter. To my mind, they're now only at the beck and call of the Fourth Court of Guatemala City. Those poor people now have the problem."

From the Darkness

"And you?" the commissioner said in a mocking tone. "You've been inactive these last few weeks, right?"

"Yes, true. But I didn't want to be. The last story of mine they published was that of March 23rd, about the inspection visit of Ubico's departmental administrator, General Serrano. Do you remember when we accompanied him to see the work on the highway and the new kitchen hospital?"[4]

"And leaving aside the García Morán case, have you got your hands on anything else to publish right now?"

"Well, for several weeks I've been wanting to publish a commentary about the granting of the Gálvez Prize to the year's best thesis in the law faculty. Someone from Amatitlán won it, to our great pride."

"Who?" asked the commissioner, surprised. "I missed that news."

"It was Vicente Díaz Samayoa, now an attorney. You know the family. They're well-known coffee farmers in the area."

"Well, would you look at that. Great that a local beat that lot from the capital."

"Yes, they chose his thesis as the best. Do you have last month's newspapers here in your office?"

"Yes," the commissioner replied, "which one?"

"Allow me..." said Jorge.

He searched for a few minutes, mumbling: "If I remember rightly... it came out in the last few days. Let's see..." At last he exclaimed: "Here it is. Shall I read it to you?"

The commissioner agreed. Jorge, in a serious and loud voice, as if reading more than just a simple news report, said:

The Gálvez Prize, a prestigious university distinction, has been obtained this year by Vicente Díaz Samayoa and Mario Monteforte Toledo.

The first prize, the gold medal, went to Díaz Samayoa for his thesis entitled 'The Juridical Thought of the XVIIIth century'. The second, the silver medal, went to Mario Monteforte Toledo for his thesis 'The Control of Exchange Rates'.

The awarding jury comprised Flavio Herrera, David Vela and

Enrique Muñoz Meany. In the latter's absence, the respective award certificate was signed separately by Messrs Vela and Herrera.

The distinction which the aforementioned professionals have been awarded includes, along with the medals that they will receive, the diplomas that will be granted to them respectively by the Dean of the Faculty of Law.

"When was it published?" was the commissioner's only comment.

"The 20th of March. Think about it. There'll be tomorrow's paper, Wednesday the fifth. And from then until the 10th, Easter Monday. And by then the news will be very old for a commentary and congratulations to come out. And with respect to the other news, that of the García Morán case, which will be a bombshell," continued Jorge, worked up, "you lot have me muzzled."

"And that's the way it'll stay until the publicity doesn't get in the way of my investigations."

"But what investigations? What are you doing? If they have an innocent man under arrest, who's the real suspect?"

"Calm down, calm down. You'll know everything in due course, not now. And then they'll come running from *El Imparcial* for your help. Just give me time."

The commissioner was right. He was still a long way off getting something concrete out of the material that the judicial investigation had thrown up, but his intuition told him he was very close to finding out by other means. The case was crying out for a police investigation. But the problem was: where to start? The commissioner had thought a thousand times that the rumours, increasingly insistent, were true. The crime had been committed inside the house. Pedro Quezada, the only remaining suspect, was innocent. He was sure of that. The rumours about Mauricia's temperament, the contradictions about the arguments between her and the deceased, the cold certainty with which she had arrived that night at the police station to denounce Pedro, the lack of conclusive evidence against the suspect and, above all, the direct accusations made by the work colleagues of Pedro and Vicente, as well as that

From the Darkness

of Don Emilio Barrera, were too unambiguous not to carry the police chief to the obvious conclusion. He had to do something, and quickly. On the other hand, without proof, the Fourth Court would finally end up freeing Pedro subject to ongoing inquiries; but God alone knows when. It's Holy Tuesday, Commissioner Flores thought to himself in the solitude of his office, the coming days are dead, yet very propitious for making these people see sense.

The commissioner got up, walked towards the door and called officers Óscar Martínez and Julio Gómez, to take advantage of the fact, as he said, that the coast was clear now that Jorge had gone.

"I'm calling you," he explained, once they were in front of him, "to tell you what our strategy is going to be over the next few days."

The officers did not say a word. They merely listened eagerly.

"My hypothesis is the following," he continued, "and I believe, in this, we are in agreement: Pedro is innocent. Bartolo's wife killed him. With the help of someone, we still don't know who. If we take gossip into account, the strongest suspect is Pedro García, the daughter's boyfriend. There's only one problem: with what we've got as a result of the judicial investigation, we're never going to know; and if we wait for them to come and confess, we'd better do it sitting down, because they're never going to appear. So what we need is to press, to force the issue a bit."[5]

Commissioner Flores paused to await a reply, for assent. The officers told him yes, they thought the same and that the proceedings were being dragged out far too long.

"Good," the commissioner continued with a smile of satisfaction, "the plan, then, is the following: a crime like this can have only three causes, passion, money, or a mixture of both. In this case there has to be some material interest, although we know nothing about this. The only thing we can do is to apply pressure so that something about it comes to light. The intellectual author and the person covering up everything here is, without doubt, the woman. We're going to interrogate her, of course, but we must be aware from the outset that we're not going to get much that way. The person who weakens under our pressure will be Mauricia's accomplice or accomplices. I'm thinking of Pedro García. We don't know if he was her lover or not; but either way he was manipulated into being involved in all this. If we manage to get him to confess, it pulls the rug out from under her feet."

"And the children?" asked officer Gómez Hernández.

"They're also important," the commissioner answered. "Let's imagine for a moment that Pedro was turned into the mother's lover... I don't even want to think about how jealous Rogelia would be. And in the case of Félix, the son, have you asked yourself why, miraculously, he never drank the poisoned water? Was it purely by chance or did someone warn him not to? Yes Gómez, you're right, it's there that this thing can fall apart for Mauricia."

"What are we going to do?" asked officer Martínez.

"Let's take the bull by the horns," the commissioner answered decisively. "Tomorrow we'll head for Mauricia's house, put the screws on her and examine the whole house. We have to make sure she gets fucking furious, that she is left on edge, that she tells her family in the evening and they get scared that we're circling around them."

"But this is only going to put her on guard and make her take precautions," objected officer Gómez.

"Yes it is," Commissioner Flores said, "her immediate reaction will be to strike fear into the family and give precise instructions. But it's one thing controlling what people do, and another very different thing controlling what they feel. Mauricia does not have any power over this, especially if she obliged them to collaborate with her in the crime. For this reason, after interrogating her, we let Wednesday and Thursday go past. On Thursday afternoon, before nightfall and when they've returned and are back together again, we swoop down on the children. That's going to tighten the noose a little more. And on Friday morning, let's go to Pedro's lodgings and interrogate him mercilessly. It has to work. Do I have your support?"

"Sure thing, Commissioner," said officer Gómez.

"So, to work."

Mauricia, ignorant of the legal twists and turns that criminal

From the Darkness

proceedings take, watched the days pass with neither grief nor glory. All she knew was that Pedro Quezada, whom she herself had accused, remained under arrest. And although she made an effort to ignore the furtive looks, the whispering behind her back, and the concealed finger-pointing, she was not unaware that the rumours against her were intensifying. She knew that her neighbours, Bartolo's family and even those who did not know her, were convinced she was the culprit. That is why it did not surprise her when she saw the resolute face of Commissioner Flores after hearing several sharp, decisive knocks on the outside gate and the dogs barking until they were out of breath. It was a visit foreseen, already long overdue. Without having thought about it consciously, Mauricia was prepared for this interrogation. Her refuge was the statements made in the initial denunciation, and she knew she must not budge one millimetre from the ideas therein.

"Good day, Mauricia," the commissioner said, and before she could answer them, "can we come in?"

"Why?" she answered with a frown, without moving to open the gate.

"We want to ask you some questions."

"I have no more to tell you. You've already questioned me once, what more do you want me to tell you?"

The commissioner, a man of experience, did not let Mauricia intimidate him. On the contrary, her boldness began to test his patience.

"Don't complicate things. Open the door immediately," he warned her.

Reluctantly, Mauricia crossed, feeling for the key to the padlock in the pockets of her apron.

"Best if we sit down," the commissioner said, collapsing into a chair in the dining room. "Take a note of everything, officer Gómez. And you, Mauricia, what are you doing standing up? I told you to sit down."

Mauricia sat at the edge of a chair, looking at the floor, her hands together and her breathing slightly agitated.

"Let's see," the commissioner said with the calmness that comes with experience, "the story that Quezada is the guilty one I know by heart. I don't want to hear another word about that, understood?"

Mauricia nodded her head, but without raising her eyes.

"Good, that way we understand each other better. Tell me, do you know that Vicente Morataya was freed because of lack of evidence against him?"

Mauricia nodded again without looking him in the eye.

"I don't want you to make faces, I want you to answer me, or have you suddenly gone mute?"

"Yes, yes, I found out a few days ago."

"Do you know what it means for a judge of first instance to have no evidence and to keep in jail someone who, with each day that passes, seems more and more innocent of what he's accused of?"

The commissioner was not expecting an answer to the question. He waited a few seconds, then continued.

"It means that the true culprit is walking about freely, mocking the law. And did you know that this angers the judges a great deal, and then they begin to go back to the case, to make inquiries, questions here and there? Mauricia," he added, moving closer to the chair and looking for her eyes, "Judge Cáceres of Guatemala City is on the verge of letting Pedro Quezada go. All he has against him is what you said. Do you realise? It's your word against his. This is going nowhere, they're going to let him go at any moment and he'll begin hunting the true culprit."

"And what's that got to do with me? I've already told you what I know."

"Don't be foolish, Mauricia," said the commissioner slowly, "perhaps you don't know what the whole town is going round saying? Don't tell me you haven't found out."

"I don't get involved with anybody. I've never joined in with the gossip of those people who spend their lives at their windows and in the shops talking about the lives of everyone else."

"Well then, allow me to keep you informed. According to them, you killed Bartolo."

"That's not true! Bartolo himself told me it had been Pedro."

"Yes, I already know that from your accusation. But, know what,

From the Darkness

the people are saying even more: according to popular rumour, Pedro García is not the boyfriend of your daughter Rogelia, but yours."

"Gossiping sons of bitches!" she spat, clearly losing control. "But don't tell me 'everyone's saying so', give me names, who are they?"

"Why do you want to know? To take reprisals?"

"What's that?"

"Vengeance."

"No, only to complain, to ask them why they're saying it, if they have any proof."

"Mauricia, this isn't an official interrogation. It's just the visit of a friend coming to prepare you. A storm is gathering. When the judge descends with all his might, they'll take you to the lower court here again and, who knows, perhaps they'll take you to the capital to answer whatever the judge wants to ask you. Believe me, this is no joke, it's very serious. Judge Cáceres is going to give you names, those who've been to talk in his ear about what they know or think they know about you: that you are an angry person, that you have a lover, that you wanted to be left with the house, that you killed Lencho, your stepson, ten years ago, and a long list of horrible things that they say about you and that are now on the judge's desk."

"They can say what they want, I'm not at fault."

"Think hard about what you're doing. I already know you won't tell me anything now. As I told you, I am coming as a friend to tell you what's what. You're a grown-up and know what you're doing. The only thing you need to know is that if you had anything to do with this business it's better to confess. And those who may have collaborated with you too. The judge will be much softer with you in that case, but he'll be very hard if he manages to ascertain that you lied. I know what I'm talking about. Think about your children. Something like that can't be hidden, it will come to light when one least expects it to and with far worse consequences than one could ever have imagined."

Mauricia again fixed her eyes on the ground. She kept her hands tautly together on her lap. It was at this point that the commissioner realised his suspicions were closer to the truth than he had thought. If beforehand he had allowed some room for doubt about Pedro, now he knew that the poor man was innocent, the victim of a calumny by this woman who was hiding the truth about her husband's murder. The question now was: Who had embarked with her on the same adventure?

"The end of Holy Week is now coming," the commissioner said, as if sermonising. "It's going to be peaceful. I want you to take your time, to think hard about what we've discussed, to explore your conscience." He continued, while signalling to officer Gómez as he wrote, "We are the judge's advance guard, we make prior inquiries so that they don't waste their time. That's why I'm here, so that the inevitable course of events harms as few people as possible. Do you understand me?"

Mauricia did not answer.

"Okay," the commissioner said, already standing, "we're off. Have a good day."

The two men walked to the door and closed it behind them.

They returned to the police barracks at once. Officer Gómez wanted to transcribe what he had just scribbled down as soon as possible.

Mauricia remained in silence, sitting in the same place lost in thought. She had never felt so alone. There were still a few hours before her family would get home. When eventually she reacted, she stood up automatically, as if to flee impulsively. Her gaze traced the complete outline of the room, trying to discover in some corner the hidden eyes of those watching her, yes, following her wherever she wanted to go. Day and night.

Félix was the first to return. But Mauricia contained herself and decided not to say anything and to wait for Pedro and Rogelia. Her head was spinning. Did they know something, and were just sounding her out? Would they have already spoken to Pedro, perhaps? And the children? Rogelia had a weak character, anything could intimidate her. Would it be her? Or perhaps Félix, who had been close to Bartolo. And what about Hilario, fearful that someone would point to him as an accomplice or even as the instigator?

When Rogelia and Pedro appeared, Mauricia sat them down at

From the Darkness

the table and told them in detail about the visit of Commissioner Flores and officer Gómez. She warned them that, sooner or later, they were also going to be questioned. She scrutinised their eyes for fear, betrayal. She told them not to worry, that they had already searched the house and not found anything, that everything was simply down to gossip. She reminded them that they had their own story and that no-one should stray a centimetre from it for any reason. She also warned them that Commissioner Flores was right and, given the situation, they would soon be summoned by the judge in the capital.

Rogelia and Pedro were dumbfounded. Unconsciously they had believed everything was over and there was nothing to fear. Why are they going round asking questions again? What more did the judge in the capital want beyond what he already had against Pedro Quezada? And, although there was no principal suspect, why had it occurred to them that the family was hiding something?

Pedro García grew scared. He tried to leave but Mauricia told him not to, that they were together in this and they had to match their stories. At one point, while Mauricia was warning them about the case, Pedro, visibly breaking, spoke of returning to the coast, saying that there was no shortage of work there. Mauricia scolded him, told him not to be stupid, this was the very worst moment to flee and, with Ubico's police, if everything was discovered there was nowhere to hide because they had eyes everywhere. And then, indeed, there would be no mercy.

Rogelia was silent as she listened to what her mother was saying. But she seemed absent, as if she was miles away, as if hearing a distant call without deciding to answer it. Suddenly, out of the blue, she interrupted her mother and asked if Félix already knew about this. Mauricia narrowed her eyes, stared at her and said: Leave your brother to me. You worry about doing what I tell you, how and when I say so. Someone has to take decisions here, and that's me, understand?

Pedro took off as soon as he could. Rogelia got on with her chores, automatically, and Mauricia shut herself in with Félix to bring him up to date with what was going on.

Oswaldo Salazar

Just as Commissioner Flores had planned, Holy Wednesday passed uneventfully. No-one came looking for them, nor did they feel they were being followed when they went into the street. Pedro did not show his face at the house for the whole day and Rogelia, hoping to see him arrive at any moment, did not go out. The only one who followed her normal routine was Mauricia. But with extreme care, of course.

Commissioner Flores remained in his quarters to give no-one anything to talk about. But he entrusted the task of keeping a close watch on Mauricia to an anonymous informant, a neighbour. The report arrived during the afternoon and was received with the secrecy that it deserved by officer Martínez, who immediately drafted a memo that had to be on the commissioner's desk before nine that evening.

It being six-thirty in the afternoon on Wednesday 5th of April 1939, I received the report on the tail placed on Mauricia Hernández, suspected of the crime committed against that person who in life had been her husband Bartolo García Morán.

Meagre in its use of language, but abundant in content, the report refers to the observations of the anonymous agent from the early hours of the morning to well into the afternoon. It places on record in its two sheets that the aforementioned Mauricia, at the start of the working day, limited herself to carrying out what appears to be her daily domestic routine. Midday also passed without major surprises. But in the afternoon, at about four, says our faithful friend, Mauricia left, wrapped in her shawl with some papers in her hand. She walked on the shaded side of the street at a standard pace, turning round to look from time to time, until going into the main streets of Cantón San Lorenzo. There she stopped at a house on the corner that, it was ascertained by asking in the nearest shop, belongs to Mr Hilario Almeda who, according to the timely and generous information given by the shop assistant there present, has lived alone at the address for as long as anyone can remember.

The informant continues by referring to the fact that Mauricia

From the Darkness

knocked repeatedly at the door, obviously annoyed by not receiving any answer and being seen doing so by passers-by. For a moment, the report says, Mauricia appeared to lean against the door as if whispering to someone who, for whatever motive, reason or circumstance, refused to open it. A few minutes later, finishes the informant, showing signs of anger through her gestures and double-quick pace, Mauricia returned to her house by the shortest route. Without more to report, Mr Commissioner, I hereby inform you about the events as and how they occurred. Yours faithfully,

Oscar Martínez
Officer of the National Police

He re-read it several times. When he was satisfied, he signed it and went to leave it on the commissioner's desk.

No-one knew when the chief would read it. For years Commissioner Flores had not followed routines, he had kept a careful eye upon his activities week in week out and, when he found a pattern, when he discovered that he was beginning to fall into a habit, he had changed. For his own safety and that of the town, he said, he would not like some sly customer to catch him off-guard just because he had followed rigid routines.

That night, one he himself had predicted would be peaceful and without news, he did not show his face. Mid-morning the following day, he arrived, in no hurry, to read officer Martínez's report. Outside, his subordinates awaited his reaction. After a short while, the door of the office opened and the commissioner called in his two star officers.

"I didn't expect this thing about Hilario," he said. "I mean," he corrected himself, "I knew this woman had to have a lover, but not one older than her husband. Who is this Mauricia, really? What is it that she really wants?"

"Well," pointed out Martínez, "we're just supposing Hilario is her lover."

"Yes," the commissioner said reflexively, "but let's hold on to this information for later, like a secret weapon. Remember," he added, jabbing his finger at them, "we haven't completed our plan."

"You're right," said officer Gómez, "today we have to seek out the children."

"I don't want you to put them under a lot of pressure," the commissioner warned. The pressure must come down upon Pedro García tomorrow. And I'll take care of that."

"How do you want us to question them?" asked Gómez.

"Nothing scandalous," he explained, "and even less so in public. I want it to be done separately. Don't go together to each one. Best split up."

"Yes, but I," Gómez said again, "I was referring to the questions. What do you want us to ask them?"

"Details," he said, with precision, "details about the day of the murder. We already know they've concocted a story. If they are deceiving us and trip over their own lies, it'll be because of details. Also ask them about their parents' relationship. I'm sure they're hiding something about that."

The officers left immediately to carry out their mission. Since Bartolo's death, Félix had been left in charge of the sowing, without problems. Officer Gómez knew that if he got there before midday he would find him bent over the earth, working. Martínez, more gifted in diplomacy, had to go to Mauricia's house to question Rogelia. Both officers knew little was expected of these interrogations, yet it was important to keep up the pressure, not in order to discover anything, but to provoke it.

In the afternoon, Commissioner Flores ordered the officers back to discuss their errands. Gómez recounted that, just as expected, he had found Félix at the pasture, and that his coldness, his near indifference in talking about his father's death, had surprised him. He recalled that the youth had become confused when asked about the relationship between his parents; that after a while, looking at the ground and frowning, he had said yes, they used to fight, but now, no; that years ago, yes, they quarrelled but, thank God, now they had found happiness. By way of finishing, Gómez said that before leaving he had warned the kid it was best to tell the truth, life is no

From the Darkness

game and if he was hiding something it would be better to say so because sooner or later everything comes to light, especially wrongdoing.

Officer Martínez, brandishing a sheet of paper on which he had taken a note of his questions, recounted that when he reached the house Mauricia had received him in a hostile manner but, not letting her intimidate him, he had told her he did not want to speak with her but with her daughter Rogelia, and alone. He went on to explain that, by now, Rogelia had already shown her face in the doorway and all he had to do was tell her he wanted her to answer some questions. Reading straight from his sheet of paper, he said he had not got any clear information out of her, that she had said her parents never fought, that there were no motives for anyone in the family to wish Bartolo dead, that she did not know whether her father had any debt or problem with anyone other than Pedro Quezada, and that it was a lie, lying gossip, the thing about Pedro, her betrothed, being her mother's lover.

The commissioner had listened to them in silence, without interrupting once. When he spoke, it was to console them, above all Martínez. I told you not to worry and that we already knew it would turn out this way. But the important thing was what, at that very moment, was going on in that house. Right now, the commissioner said, they're updating Pedro García. He paused and then, with a smile, continued, saying: That bastard is not going to sleep all night. And tomorrow we'll swoop down on him at the farm. We'll take the opportunity to scrutinise the place carefully and ask the workers and tenants questions here, there and everywhere.

On Good Friday, the 7th of April, the day dawned cloudy. When officers Gómez and Martínez arrived at the police station, the chief was already waiting for them. It was a highly unusual day, one of religious traditions and time off work. Many people made the journey to the capital to see the icon of the Lord of Mercy and the processions of the Holy Burial. People were sad, the streets empty and the houses locked. On the farms, and above all those where the workers lived, there was an atmosphere of peace, of rest.

Oswaldo Salazar

The commissioner was sure of finding Pedro García in the unmarried quarters of the Rancho Grande farm owned by Adolfo Mazariegos and situated within the Amatitlán jurisdiction.

They found him collapsed in a hammock rocking to and fro calmly as it was pushed reluctantly by the warm, faint wind that barely flicked the tops of the trees and the women's hair. He was not alone, but accompanied by several work colleagues talking and from time to time laughing among themselves.

On seeing the three policemen heading towards them, the group interrupted its chatter and some, the youngest, stood up. Pedro García was the last to turn and see what was going on. The commissioner and his two officers had approached him from behind.

"Pedro García Gesenäuer!" the commissioner called in a clear voice.

Those of his friends who had not stood finally did so and reflexively fell back a few steps. The commissioner's presence intimidated them. Pedro turned to look with difficulty, shading his eyes with his hand because the morning light dazzled him. At first, the three men appeared to his eyes as no more than blurred shadows. But the voice of Commissioner Flores and his ever decreasing distance at last enabled him to make out the feared face of authority.

"Good day," answered Pedro, uncertain, "what can I do for you?"

"Much more than you think, Pedro García," said the commissioner, in a tone of threatening camaraderie.

Pedro stood up. Suddenly he found himself at the centre of a circle. His friends remained all around expectantly, with long faces and tightly shut mouths.

"Gentlemen," the commissioner said, looking at them fixedly, "take a hike. We're going to talk to Pedro."

Without a word, the men began to spread out in all directions, turning to watch and commenting about it to each other.

"Wouldn't it be better to go into this cabin where it's quieter?" suggested officer Gómez.

"Yes," the commissioner agreed, without turning to look at him. "You first, Pedro."

The shed, criss-crossed by rays of sunlight that entered through

From the Darkness

the cracks in the tiles, was damp and smelled of smoke from firewood.

Pedro directed them to his bunk and offered them a seat. The two officers sat in front of him, and the only one to remain on his feet in the midst of the scene was Commissioner Flores.

"You're not going to tell me you don't know why we're here," the commissioner said as his opening shot. "Eh?" he asked, lowering his head and looking Pedro in the eyes. "Sure you know, and you've even been expecting it all this time? We've already questioned the Hernández García family: Mauricia, your girlfriend Rogelia, and Félix too. You know that, and it scares you to think about it because you're never going to know exactly what they told us."

"Yes, I imagine..." stuttered Pedro.

"This isn't anything imaginary. We're talking about murder here, about the death of a man to whom you owed money and were unable to pay."

Gómez and Martínez looked at each other in surprise. This was nothing more than a rumour, it had been supposed, and now the commissioner was referring to it as if he had hard evidence of it in his hand, no less, as if all he needed to do was to show this to the suspect.

Pedro was a weak man, extremely thin, with a delicate constitution, a long face and Caucasian features that gave him a mystical air. A deep sadness was reflected in his wild eyes and half-open mouth, empty of words.

"Nothing to say?" asked the commissioner.

"Are you accusing me of Don Bartolo's death?" Pedro reacted, on seeing the glum expression of the policemen.

"Stop messing about. In your situation I wouldn't beat about the bush. The judge in the capital has already let Vicente go and is about to free Pedro Quezada. There's nothing against them."

"But... I don't know anything about this..." he stammered.

"That poor man was poisoned, he died worse than a dog. He was given insecticide. Someone has to be guilty."

"But Pedro Quezada wanted to kill him..."

"Yes, but we've already proved it wasn't him. You, however..." he said, pausing, "have much to explain."

"About the money?" he asked.

"That's one thing," the commissioner said, drawing close to Pedro's face. "But first you have to explain why you didn't tell us about it when we questioned you. Were you hiding it? Why didn't you want us to know? How could you imagine we weren't going to find out? Everyone knows about it, and everyone is saying this really was a reason for killing the poor old man."

"No! I was saving up to pay him."

"And in the meantime screwing his woman?"

"What? I'm the fiancé of Rogelia, the daughter."

"Just imagine what we have here for Judge Cáceres in the capital. Nothing less than an open and shut case. The culprit who had the motives: debt and adultery. And, what's more, who wanted to cover it all up, but was discovered by everyone. Even worse, who continues to deny it without being able to prove his innocence. Fuck you, little Pedro! This means the firing squad. And for us," he added, turning to look at his subordinates, "promotion!"

Their laughter resounded and was followed by some quips and, finally, by an icy, expectant silence that left Pedro alone on an empty stage.

"Listen," the commissioner said in a paternal way, "I'm going to tell you the way things are: Have you heard that nonsense about justice being blind? Have you seen the statuettes of the woman with her eyes covered holding scales in her hand as if she were in the market? Well, what this means is that, to the figure of justice, no matter who it may be, it doesn't matter a shit if Tom, Dick or Harry is guilty. What matters is that there's a culprit. And because that's the way things are, let me tell you, you're the most obvious candidate. If I send a dispatch to Judge Fuentes Novella with what I've been telling you in it, he's going to see a way out of the hole he's in. And for him, too, solving this problem is going to be a triumph. To put things another way: we all gain something from this, and the only one that gets trodden on is you."

Pedro said nothing. He was just there with his open mouth tracing a mute, half smile, being driven crazy, and looking at the faces of the policemen as if appealing for help without knowing what to say.

From the Darkness

Commissioner Flores turned to look at his officers, stood back, folded his arms and said:

"So that's it? You've got nothing to say? I know, you're thinking that it's not worth confessing because you're going to be fucked either way. Fine," he continued, bending forward slightly, "it's not like that. If you tell me everything now and, for my part, I say you collaborated with the authorities in every possible way to allow us to best fulfil our sacred duty, Judge Cáceres is going to treat you better, he's going to give you a milder punishment. If you want my advice, I'm telling you that this is what you should do. If not, they're going to condemn you anyway, but under the worst circumstances."

"I said 'No'," babbled Pedro, mumbling, "that she should look for help somewhere else, but she made me…"

"What did you say? Speak up, because we can't understand you," said officer Gómez, drawing close to Pedro and taking off his hat.

The commissioner put his hand on the detective's shoulder as if to tell him not to put the man under any more pressure, he had begun to confess and it was better to let him get everything out on his own.

From the Darkness

VII

*I*t being twelve-thirty on the 9th day of April 1939 in Guatemala City and in the presence of the Judge and Secretary, Colonel Manuel Arriola Cabrera, the Chief of Number One Police Barracks, in whose previous legal oath it was stated is 43 years old, married, a native of El Progreso, a resident of this city domiciled in the Barracks where he exercises his office, affirms that the following persons from Amatitlán were received at this Barracks by an order of the General Police Directorate carried out by the Investigation Department: Pedro Francisco García Gesenäuer, Félix Hernández García, Rogelia Hernández García and Mauricia Hernández Urbina; and that he sent the two women to the Women's Prison, and that the two men are being kept in this Barracks for all legal purposes.*

Thus read the judicial record written hurriedly by the secretary of the Fifth Court of First Instance, B. González, a man who never ceased to be surprised by the things he saw. Judge Portillo had asked the colonel to, please, wait a few minutes for the secretary to finish writing out the record that allowed them to undertake the due procedure within the barracks itself. At this point, no-one had remembered about Pedro Quezada being processed for the same crime by the Fourth Court of First Instance, still shut away in the shadows awaiting a miracle. Colonel Arriola Cabrera's frown revealed the officer's impatience over the testing procedures of these pettifogging lawyers, always so disposed to complicating everything.

At last they left. And such was their haste that, within just half an hour, they were already confronting the accused. Before leaving, Colonel Arriola had given precise instructions about bringing the two females from the women's prison. There could be no delay. It was essential for the judge to interrogate all of them in one go and he must not be left running about from side to side.

Judge Portillo was astonished when he saw the four enter. Pedro, Rogelia and Félix had their heads bowed, not daring to look him in the eye. But Mauricia was arrogant, and this was reflected in her expression, the hardest he had ever seen. He observed their poor, frayed and crumpled clothes, those of peasants.

Colonel Arriola Cabrera made them line up against the wall. Still without saying anything, the judge looked at them there, silent, their hands tied behind their backs; he heard the murmur of the reporters and photographers outside who wanted to enter to be the first to get the scoop and, looking at the colonel, said:

"Let's start with him, what his name?"

The colonel did not answer, but turned his face and said in a loud voice:

"Everyone out except García Gesenäuer."

Of course, "out" did not mean to go out and fall into the hands of the anxious journalists, but rather that they were to be taken to a room used for eating in.

Secretary González, who had come all the way carrying a typewriter, was already seated at a small wooden table that rocked as he began to put in the paper.

"Whenever you want," he said to the judge as he inserted a sheet of stamped paper, carbon and a flimsy blue sheet to take a copy of the interrogation.

"Let's start," said the judge. "Sit down, please."

"No!" interrupted Colonel Arriola, forcefully. "That bastard remains standing. You sit, Attorney."

Pedro was pale, he had the aspect of a sick man, weak by nature, and his attitude looked like one of absolute submission. He was the

From the Darkness

typical culprit who has confessed, who does not look one in the eye, answers by mumbling in a low voice with incomplete phrases, has neither alibi nor justification, nor even motives for being there and, moreover, imagines that the matter is not serious and soon he will walk free because it was never his intention to hurt anyone.

The interrogation began, and the secretary did not intend to miss a word on that historic occasion. Like everyone else, he had never seen anything like it. It was monstrous: An entire family conspiring to murder the head of the household. What a state of affairs. Where were the Devil's ways leading us, he thought as he watched and listened to that impassive man who seemed incapable of hurting a fly yet had murdered his future father-in-law, no more nor less than his second father, and he did not note any remorse whatsoever in him. Shameless, the secretary thought, he deserves to die. And whilst his conscience toyed with the accused before him, Secretary González automatically drafted the heading of the interrogation by referring to a pile of dirty, crumpled papers that were the personal documents of Pedro Francisco García Gesenäuer. With the proficiency of habit, the secretary could learn from them straight away that Pedro was just 29 years old and that it was true, as he himself said and everyone had testified, that he was single, a farmhand and had been born in San Lucas, Sacatepéquez, but, at the time of the crime, was resident in Amatitlán. He verified also, as he had done in his years as an assistant, that, like so many thousands of others in this country of bastards, he thought, Pedro was the love child of Carlos García and Cornelia Gesenäuer; that he was a reserve soldier who, at least according to the report of the judiciary, had never been arrested, detained or had proceedings taken against him. On this point, Secretary González stopped for a moment under the impatient gaze of his honour, the judge. Something was missing.

"What's up?" the judge asked with an inquisitorial look.

"It doesn't say anywhere if the accused has any known nickname," answered the secretary, bewildered.

"So, ask him."

The secretary raised his eyes and found the bowed head of Pedro, who shook it without saying a word.

"You have to declare it verbally," he told him.

"No, they don't call me anything," he answered in a resigned tone.

"Fine," said the judge, "now it's my turn. Let's get through this as quickly as possible. Tell me," he continued, directing himself to Pedro, "what you know about the death of Mr García Morán."

Pedro cleared his throat slightly, and said:

"What I know is what everyone there in Amatitlán knows."

"And what is that?"

"Well, that they poisoned Don Bartolo and that on the night of the same day as the murder they went and had Pedro Quezada brought from his house after accusing him of being responsible."

"And what else?" the judge cross-examined him. "According to the police record, you have something to say with respect to this accusation, right?"

"Yes," he answered, lowering his eyes again. "Pedro Quezada is innocent. They blamed the death on him only because it is said that he and Bartolo became enemies some time ago."

"So? Which person or persons killed Bartolo García?"

"It was all of us."

"Explain yourself, give your statement some detail."

"Several days beforehand, one night that I arrived early to see Rogelia. Mrs Mauricia Hernández, Don Bartolo's wife, all confused, took me aside to another room and begged me to get her some insecticide because she wanted to kill her husband. As you can imagine, I was dumbfounded, without knowing what to say but, and I don't know why, perhaps in the hope of making an impression, without thinking about what I was doing, I did my best to get it. But I couldn't steal a little of what they use on the farm until the thirteenth. That evening I took it to her and she thanked me very much. But it wasn't until the 15th, when I went to the house for a short while, that she told me she'd already given him the toxin mixed up with three poisonous larvae she'd added herself and he was in hospital. So I went there and, on the slope leading up to it, I met Félix, the son, who told me with a long pale face that his dad had already died. I came back with him so he could tell me what had happened. And when we got there, to my surprise, Mrs Mauricia, without anyone

From the Darkness

noticing, confirmed to me with a smile that she already knew Don Bartolo had expired."

"Let's see," said the judge, adjusting himself on his mahogany chair, "let's go back in time a bit. Tell me how and by what means you obtained the poison."

"I drew it from a pot that's on the Rancho Grande farm of Don Adolfo Mazariegos. I was working there as a farmhand and sometimes it fell to me to scrub livestock with the insecticide. That's why I knew where to get it from. The problem was for no-one to see me. And it wasn't until the 13th, at the end of the morning, that I was left alone for a while in the storeroom where they keep it. I took the chance to grab some in a little bottle."

"Which person or persons," asked the judge leaning his head forward and frowning, "knew that you and Mauricia Hernández planned to kill Bartolo García?"

"The children," answered Pedro, who then thought further. "Well, as far as I know, only Rogelia. And I say this because I was present, on the night of the 14th, when madam Mauricia arrived with Rogelia and told her I had something important to tell her. Then, as best I could and surprised at it having to be me, I told her everything, what her mother had asked me for, that I had then obtained the poison, etcetera; and then she, Mauricia, told her a whole lot of stuff while Rogelia, poor thing, cried and cried without understanding a thing."

"And Félix, the son?" asked the judge, interrupting Pedro's recollections.

"He was inside. At that point he wasn't aware of it. Later, when Don Bartolo was already dead and Mrs Mauricia had made it clear to us what we could say, Rogelia told me they'd told Félix on the day when they were about to leave for work in the field so that he wouldn't drink from the same gourd."

"To what end was this crime committed?" asked the judge. He paused and scratched his head. "Put another way, why did you do it?"

"I've already told you," replied Pedro, calmly. "I don't know. All that occurs to me is that I did it so as not to contradict Mrs

Mauricia. Anyone can tell you I never had problems with Don Bartolo. We always had a good relationship."

"Fine," said the judge in a conclusive tone, "to finish up tell us when, where and by whom you were detained."

"It was on Friday at about five in the afternoon, in Amatitlán. The police inspector arrived in person with two officers."

There was a pause and no-one moved. All eyes lingered on Judge Portillo, who said nothing. Suddenly, energetically, like a call to attention, Colonel Arriola Cabrera asked:

"Have you finished with him now, attorney?"

"Yes," he answered, "now he can go. Bring the next one in."

"Which out of all of them?"

"The other boy," he said. "In that way, when we've finished they can be taken to their cells and we'll remain alone with the women."

"Take the accused to his cell," said the colonel, taking Pedro's arm, "and bring me the other one, the kid. But right now, not tomorrow, bastards!" he shouted.

Pedro left silently, walking slowly, staring at the ground. When he left the door remained open and the judge could see his skinny, almost imperceptible figure disappearing down the corridor on the way to his cell.

Some time passed. At last, Félix appeared at the door. His hands were tied and his brow furrowed. It struck the judge that there was no regret, not even any emotion, in this youth.

The interrogation began, and in a clear sharp tone, as if speaking about something of no real concern to him, Félix said he was 15 years of age, a farmer, a native of Amatitlán, the natural son of Bartolo García Morán and Mauricia Hernández Urbina, and had no known nickname.

When the judge asked him if he knew the deceased and what relationship he had had with him, Félix, quite sure of himself, answered that he had been his father and, perhaps for that reason, he had loved him as a son does, their relationship had been very good.

The judge then asked him to relate what he knew about the motives behind the death of his father Bartolo. To which Félix

From the Darkness

replied that he knew his father had died from poisoning by his mother who had put poison in the water prepared by García Gesenäuer; that, together, they had gone to work and his mother had warned him not to drink it; that he had kept this news to himself, watched as his father drank the poison and did not tip him off; and that, within a short while, he had begun to complain of a strong colic and his mother, who was nearby, ran over and they took him to their house.

By now tiring, the judge asked him the token question, to say by whom, where and at what time he had been detained. To which Félix answered the previous night, in Amatitlán, by a police inspector and two officers.

And to finish, the judge wanted to know where the container for the poison was. He answered that, on his mother's instructions, he himself had broken the fateful gourd.

Pedro García's statement had just been corroborated by Félix. It was not until now that the judge and secretary had actually begun to have a case. It was all falling into place. According to Colonel Arriola Cabrera, the accused had been kept completely incommunicado from the moment the first of them had begun to sing. It had been impossible for them to come to a prior agreement. Moreover, it would have been absurd for them to do so in order to confess. There was no doubt, this was the truth about the García Morán case.

Next it was Rogelia's turn. Mauricia, according to Judge Portillo, had to be last, she was the main course. Colonel Arriola agreed. Her story should tie together all the previous statements.

Rogelia Hernández García stated that she was 17 years of age, single, did domestic work, was a native and resident of Amatitlán, the natural daughter of Bartolo García Morán and Mauricia Hernández Urbina; she recounted that she had been detained the previous night, in Amatitlán, by two police officers. She added that, yes, she knew Pedro García Gesenäuer, him being her betrothed, that she also knew Bartolo, her father when he was alive, and that all she knew about his death was what had occurred on the 15th of March at about three in the afternoon in the Amatitlán hospital. The judge asked if that meant she had not been aware that her father was going to be murdered; to which she replied, hanging her head and letting her tangled and dirty hair fall over her face, that yes, that the truth is yes, she had found out one day before from her boyfriend Pedro, who had spoken about it to her on his own behalf and on behalf of her mother Mauricia, and had told her that they had everything ready for the following day.

The judge, seeking associations that would make the case logical, cross-examined her by asking if she knew what type of poison they were going to give him. To which the accused answered that on the night of the 14th, Pedro, her boyfriend, in the silent presence of her mother Mauricia, had shown her a kind of small, pink bottle telling her that it was insecticide and no-one could survive something like that. Judge Portillo, increasingly animated by his findings, and ready to finish off because he had by now learned enough, asked if she had watched her father Bartolo and her brother Félix march off to work on the morning of the 15th of March taking with them the fatal potion. After a silence, as if she was receiving a visit from ghosts she was acquainted with, the declarant said that she did not see them when they left, but that she had been unable to sleep and remembered perfectly that she had heard every sound made by her mother when she had got up earlier than usual, at about five in the morning, to prepare the poisoned water that would end her father's life.

Judge Portillo paused and the colonel, now familiar with what he considered the ridiculous way attorneys have of interrogating prisoners and witnesses, assumed that Rogelia would not, for now, have anything more to declare. He made a guard take her somewhere away from any journalist and gave precise instructions that at the same time they should bring in the main prisoner, Mauricia Hernández Urbina.

Secretary González made himself comfortable in his chair, arranged the paper, checked if he had enough material so as not to interrupt the interrogation with things that were not important, and set to waiting for the accused to enter. They said that she had confessed, that she had done it with a coldness that froze the blood. It was, however, the first time she would have to make a judicial

From the Darkness

declaration itself. A declaration that they had to improvise, that had caught them unprepared and, as they say, with their trousers down.

Like the previous accused, Mauricia also entered after a few minutes, her hands tied behind her back and a guard holding her by the arm. But she was not looking at the ground, nor did she appear impassive. Her expression was haughty, intransigent, betraying bottled-up anger, a radical rebelliousness against any form of masculine authority. And there she was, amidst a group of men, each representing instances of judgement, custody, of the recording and archiving of her every word as if taking an account of her defiant acts so as to make her pay for them later in an unknown way.

Without waiting for the judge's order, Secretary González began to type out the heading of the statement. It was the moment everyone – officials, jurists, and assistants – had been waiting for. From memory, fingers flying across the keyboard and without taking his eyes off her, the secretary wrote down what he had already seen in Mauricia's personal papers: that she was 30 years old, just one year more than Pedro, he thought with a certain masculine malice; that, as ever, she was considered a 'single' housewife, a daughter outside matrimony like almost everyone else, and pure Amatitlánecan.

There was a moment of silence and all eyes turned toward Judge Portillo.

"Let's begin at the end," he said, amid general anticipation. "Tell us Mauricia, at what time, in what place and by what person or what persons you were detained."

Her rigid expression, thin lips and hard gaze strained to pronounce, at last, the first words since her capture.

"It was yesterday in the morning," she said in a confident and sharp tone. "A police officer arrived at the house and told me he'd come to detain me over Bartolo's death."

"Bartolo who, specifically?" cross-examined the judge, seeking to leave no loose ends.

"Bartolo García Morán, my husband. Who else was it going to be?" she said to the astounded looks of those present.

"If you're so sure about what you're declaring," said the judge, reclining in his chair and in a mocking tone, "let's see, tell us if you know when, where and how Bartolo García died."

"And why wouldn't I know," she answered, "if it was me myself who prepared the poison so he'd drink it in the water in the gourd he took to work every day."

"Yes, okay," commented the judge, turning with a smile to look at his colleagues, "but we want to know how you did it."

Mauricia, for the first time, lowered her eyes; but not with the intention of assuming any guilt, but of remembering, of recounting the course of events.

"On my orders," she said, pausing briefly, "Pedro García, my daughter's betrothed, whom we considered a friend, brought me a little insecticide because I had asked him for it insistently. By his own hand, he poured it into the empty gourd the night before. That was the 14th day of March. Later, without anyone discovering, when they were all asleep, I added to the poison three larvae that I'd ground down on a brick near the stone hearth. I left it there ready so that the following day, as always, Bartolo would pour water into the gourd and take it with him to work."

"Tell me," said the judge, hesitating, "why you poisoned your husband, with what purpose."

"Because by then I was tired," she replied with a conviction that came from deep within. "Because by then I couldn't bear the mistreatment he had inflicted upon us for years. My children have scars, he left them all marked by the thrashings he gave them. And me too, he hit me like a piece of timber, to leave you like new he would say to me, and it took me days, weeks to recuperate, hiding my face from people, greeting them half-heartedly so they didn't ask questions or gossip. It was horrible. And it went on for years, almost as long as I can remember. I don't know how I put up with so much. But finally the day came when I said no more, and everything ended."

She had spoken out for herself, as if in a spontaneous confession with regard for neither judge nor confessor and, without exception, those present were frozen like stone, listening to those forthright, precise words, and not knowing whether they were facing a crimi-

From the Darkness

nal or a victim. After a moment's silence, the judge, furtively reviewing his sheet of notes, asked:

"What was it that you warned your son Félix about before he left for work with his father on the morning of the 15th of March?"

"I took him to my room," said Mauricia, now assuming a different manner, "and there I told him everything, that things couldn't go on as they were, that for his own good and everyone else's he had to help me, that he didn't have to do anything, just agree not to try the water from the gourd and let Bartolo drink it without saying anything, that it was going to be unpleasant but it was best to get the worst over quickly, to endure it and only do what I was going to tell him to."

"And him?" interrupted the judge.

"There he stayed, quiet, as mute as ever. I was scared, his silence always frightened me. Sure he remembered the way Bartolo treated us; but also, by then, for a while he had been going with him day-in day-out to work in the fields and scrub. That's why I was never sure about his reaction. I didn't want him to turn against me, tell Bartolo everything and then have him come and kick me to death."

At last she had displayed some fear. This made the judge feel more confident in himself and in the interrogation he was undertaking in full view of his entire team.

"Who else had prior knowledge of what you were planning to do?"

"Well," she said, raising her eyes and trying to remember, "as well as Pedro and my son Félix, only Rogelia. Pedro and I told her one night before. She saw the bottle with insecticide that Pedro brought from the farm where he worked. She cried a lot, she didn't know what to say; but she didn't worry me much. Pedro was there to give me a hand. Moreover, there are no misunderstandings between women. I knew, and she also knew, that we both wanted Bartolo off our backs. It's precisely as I'm telling you. That's why I hugged her and told her she knew exactly what I was feeling and there was no other way. At the end, she was calming down and then I left her to Pedro, as you know, for him to comfort her."

"Moving on to something else," said the judge, eager for conclusive evidence, "do you know where the gourd of poisoned water was left?"

"In the pasture."

"Can you be more explicit?"

"What happened was that Bartolo, as well as he could by then, when he realised the water was poisoned, between his moans and groans and in the middle of his anguish about dying, told me to destroy it so none of his children would drink from it by mistake. Then I ordered my son Félix to smash it to pieces against a stone."

"And several moments before," inquired Judge Portillo, "when Bartolo drank from the gourd, where were you?"

"At the same farm where Bartolo was working, the Sabana Grande, about two or three plots away. I'd gone with the excuse of cutting tomatoes. Truth is, I was frightened Félix was going to say something to him; that's why I followed them. So there I was, waiting for the moment. Finally, I heard his groans, approached, and the first thing he said to me was that the water had a strange colour, that he'd been poisoned for sure. He was dying, his agony had begun, and although I had planned everything, I felt scared, it filled me with dread the way death came and dragged one from this world, helplessly, without another turn of the page as they say. There was the man who'd done so much damage to me, squirming in pain like a poisoned rat dragging himself along trying to escape something that by then couldn't be cured. I don't know how much time passed. Félix, who was the only one with me, helped. We took him to the house, helping him to walk with one on one side and one on the other. When we arrived, Rogelia opened the door with a look of fright on her face that I'd never seen before. We took him to the bed and, seeing his condition, I told Rogelia to go and look for the doctor from the hospital. I did it so she wouldn't see, poor thing. He was very sick. After a while she returned with Doctor Rodríguez Padilla. At first when he came in he was very confident; but later he got scared. Yes, seeing him like that, throwing up blood and crying out in pain, made the little doctor panic. He told us he had to take him to hospital and then I went with him, there in the same carriage that he'd arrived in. Later, after a few hours, as you already know too well Mr Judge, Bartolo died."

Again, the account had left everyone silent. In the air hung the

From the Darkness

echo of those words, in the memory, the images of those expressions, the extreme designs that the imagination can assume.

"Did anyone else take part? Please answer with the same honesty that you've been talking to us with today," said the judge, offering a tribute to the courage behind this confessional tale.

"No-one else," she replied immediately. "Only Pedro, my children and I are responsible. That's why," she added, lowering her eyes, "I just want to say that there's one man, he's called Pedro Quezada, who's under arrest for no reason. He had nothing to do with this. You've no reason to be suspicious of him just because I told the police he'd had problems with my late husband."

These words did not have the same level of conviction as the account of the crime. They seemed a pale performance of something rehearsed, something that both she and Pedro were obliged to declare in the hope of easing the punishment that would be imposed on them.

The judge could not think of any other questions that would aid further in clarifying the crime against Bartolo García Morán. As a straightforward judicial interrogation, the first that had been made after the collective family confession to police chiefs, it had been very good. Now, doubts would arise that demanded some amplification of the initial statements. The day had been most unusual: it is not every day that a group of murderers and accomplices, all prepared to confess and to systematically recount the same story, is brought in.

Judge Portillo and Secretary González were exhausted. All they wanted was for the process to follow its normal bureaucratic course. Right now, there were several things to do. Pedro Quezada, for example, should be freed as soon as possible, subject to an outcome in the inquiry, clearly. Defence attorneys for the accused also had to be appointed. But both were aware that this would have to be done in the Fourth Court of First Instance, the dependency in which the case had originally been opened. They had to send the interrogation documentation to Judge Cáceres as soon as possible.

"Who do you think could do this little job?"[6] Judge Portillo asked his secretary as they were returning to their own judicial quarters.

"Remember, here in the capital no-one does anything if they don't have the state's backing."

"I don't know," the secretary answered distinterestedly. "It will have to be one of those boffins and, moreover, someone keen to make a name for himself as quickly as possible."

"Yes," said the judge, looking at the sky, "whoever represents these defendants is going to be famous. This case is going to be sensational. But it's not us who have to worry about that right now. Someone will have to do all that when the time comes."

The judge was right. The Bartolo García case was destined to become one of the most notorious in the country's judicial history. For that reason, both he and his secretary, and any other authority figure who would eventually become involved in the case, did not want to leave any loose ends, inquiries undone, deadlines unmet and, above all, urgent formalities unattended.

So, the following day, the 10th of April, at three in the afternoon, copies of the documentation from the interrogation carried out the previous day were received by the Fourth Court. Signed both by Secretary González and Judge Portillo, the documents recognised from the outset their own tribunal's lesser competence and, in an act of contrition, acknowledged fully that it was the Fourth Court that should have been conducting the case from the start. Thus was remitted, with all the indifference of an impersonal and preconceived use of language, the irrefutable evidence – as clear as the light of day – from a collective and supposedly voluntary confession.

On the 11th of April, in its first act since regaining the case, the Fourth Court of First Instance ordered the conditional release of Pedro Quezada Morales. There was no motive, now, for keeping him in prison, since the same people who had accused him at the beginning had confessed to being the culprits. Judge Cáceres was aware that when the news came out, the journalists would have many questions, among them: What have you done in relation to the man who was originally accused falsely by the true murderer? The judge wanted to be able to reply that he was freed immediately and could now be found in Amatitlán with his family, enjoying his liberty. The Man sees and hears everything, thought the judge, and rapid and

From the Darkness

efficient action could get me a promotion within the judicial system.

For Judge Cáceres, the 10th and 11th of April were days of working late and sleeplessness. The case was resolved, but now came the process that would establish the differences, the subtle nuances that would determine the guidelines and measure by which to dispense justice so as to give each what they deserved, depending on their level of participation in the crime. It was clear that the intellectual and material author of the crime was Mauricia. It was also clear that Pedro García and the children were her accomplices. Moreover, it was obvious that, in general terms, the children (and especially Félix) bore less responsibility than Pedro. The problem facing Judge Cáceres could be reduced to establishing with clarity what Pedro's real level of participation had been and, consequently, what type of punishment he should impose on him when all was said and done. He reviewed, a thousand times, the papers on which his initial declaration had been written, listed in his memory all the details of the interrogation that he had read and re-read and, papers in hand, discussed the case with the police authorities involved, Commissioner Flores and Colonel Arriola. Both had questioned the prisoners extra-judicially and, perhaps for this reason, would have some other piece of information that could throw light upon the generalisations Pedro had stated on Sunday the 9th.

On the afternoon of Monday the 10th, a few minutes before he was due to go home – the papers to free Quezada were already there on his desk ready for the following day – Secretary Schlesinger, a great fan of the police novels that had been fashionable in the United States for several years, knocked on the judge's office door and asked for permission to enter.[7] The judge asked him to come in and take a seat. As timid as he was, the secretary, with the copies of the judicial interrogation in his hand, said:

"I don't know if you've already realised, your honour, but I've been looking again at these papers and there's a significant omission about Pedro."

"Let's see," said the judge, sitting down, "tell me, because I've read them a thousand times and I can't see anything new."

"The thing is, according to Pedro, he only obtained the insecticide and Mauricia prepared everything; but when she refers to this situation, she says clearly that she only ground down the poisonous larvae and dropped them in the gourd that Pedro had already prepared with the insecticide. As it would seem, they left it like that, without water, because Bartolo was accustomed to filling it every morning before going to work."

"That's right!" said the judge, astonished. "I hadn't spotted that detail. That means we can consider Pedro García not only as an accomplice but as a material author of the crime. This changes things completely."

"But for the time being," the secretary said, "it's no more than a working hypothesis. We need evidence. What shall we do, a witness confrontation?"

"No," said the judge, "it's still not time for that. That's done only when there is an evident contradiction, that is, when a defendant or witness says white and the other says black. But if memory serves me, Pedro didn't say that he did not pour the poison into the gourd. He simply omitted it. Perhaps it was just an oversight."

"One thing's certain," the secretary added, "that this man doesn't know what's coming if he admits that he put the poison in."

"And if we want to get to the bottom of this matter," said the judge, moving closer to the secretary in an attitude of complicity, "let's make him confess now, before an attorney comes along to complicate things by advising him to tell lies."

"It's not a problem," the secretary explained. "After all, the initial declaration remains open and we can expand on it whenever we want."

"Yes," said the judge, "but nor is it wise to wait too long. In a few days we'll have to name defence counsel. Moreover, I don't know how long the police want to keep this situation under wraps. We can't delay for too long. And when it gets out and the journalists come along seeking information, we must be as clear as we can about the situation."

"Tomorrow, Tuesday the 11th, Pedro Quezada goes free," said Secretary Schlesinger, calculating. "With that, I think, we've enough to demonstrate that we're doing everything required of us in the best possible way…"

From the Darkness

"So why don't we summon Pedro García for tomorrow also?" asked the judge, interrupting his secretary's thoughtful parleying.

"Yes, that's the best thing to do, before things get more distorted by rumours and meddling by third parties," the secretary agreed.

"In that case, I'm going to be a bother," said the judge, standing up. "Before leaving, take the trouble to draft the order for the amplification of a statement. That way we can get to the barracks early tomorrow and do it."

The following day, after signing the papers for Pedro Quezada's conditional release and handing him over to his family, Judge Cáceres and Secretary Schlesinger left for the Number One Barracks of the national police. They hoped to take by surprise a Pedro García resigned to confessing the whole truth, albeit without knowing the ultimate consequences of his words.

The procedure would last an hour at most. Colonel Arriola received them grudgingly. He knew that sooner or later they would arrive to disturb the peace at his penal dominion, but he had never imagined it would be so quickly.

"Come on in," he said. "Sit down. I imagine you don't want to speak to me, but to one of the accused."

"You imagine correctly, Colonel," the judge said, surprising the secretary with his confidence. "We want to expand on Pedro García's statement. Here's the order."

"All I can I say," the colonel muttered, "is why the fuck don't you ask all the questions in one go. Let's see, bring García Gesenäuer," he shouted through the half-open door.

Pedro entered the office in a submissive manner. The judge stood up immediately and greeted the prisoner, informing him that they were not going to keep him for long, that they only wanted to expand on his declaration of the 9th of April with a few questions, and not to worry. This time, Pedro sat down and Colonel Arriola did not say anything.

JUDGE: Pedro, do you want to explain to us who arrested you in the name of the law and what you were informed at that moment?

Oswaldo Salazar

ACCUSED: *I remember it perfectly, it was the very Amatitlán commissioner of police himself, Mr Francisco Flores, and yes, if I remember right, I recall that he told me he was going to drive me to the police prison for being a suspect in the crime against Bartolo García Morán.*

JUDGE: *Can you tell us in more detail about your participation in the preparation of the lethal concoction on the night of the 14th of March?*

ACCUSED: *I already told you, it was I who took the insecticide in a little bottle.*

JUDGE: *Is that all? Did you confine yourself just to taking the poison and, from then on, everything else was left in the hands of Mauricia Hernández Urbina?*

ACCUSED: *Not exactly. While she was busying herself discussing it with Rogelia, she asked me to put the contents of the bottle into the gourd which I already knew was the one Bartolo used. So I went to the corner of the passage where they placed the gourds, made sure no-one could see me, and put it in.*

JUDGE: *Is that all? Are you saying that the poison was, when all's said and done, the only poison that was put into the gourd?*

ACCUSED: *No. Mauricia told me that she was going to add some larvae.*

The judge thanked Pedro with a broad smile of satisfaction etched across his face. He had just established the necessary facts to be able to clearly place the responsibility of everyone involved.

They said goodbye to Colonel Arriola Cabrera, not without first warning him, because of his complaints, that they could return at any moment depending on the needs of the investigation. They did not imagine that a few hours later, during the course of the afternoon, they would be back – but this time at the behest of the colonel himself.

At about midday, nearly at the time the court closed because the staff went out for lunch, the telephone rang. It was Colonel Arriola, calling as soon as he had been able to, excusing himself, to say that his colleague from Amatitlán, Commissioner Francisco Flores, had paid him a routine visit and had taken the opportunity to bring him

From the Darkness

the police record of the days during which Pedro Quezada had been under arrest. I thought, said the colonel, that we were just dealing with more rubbish, you know, these mountains of paper that tell you nothing and just take up space. What's more, I thought the commissioner just wanted to dump any remaining baggage in the case, to get rid of it. But – you're not going to believe this – imagine my surprise when I heard that an investigating agent from the police station, previously assigned to keeping Mauricia under surveillance as she went about her daily business, had reported that the confessed criminal had made a mysterious visit to a corner house inhabited by a single man. In that moment, your honour, without knowing how, many things became clear to me. No, I tell a lie, in reality just one thing became clear, but a fundamental one. And that's that, during all this time, I don't know if you've taken note, your honour, and if you have I beg your pardon, I've been bothered, vexed, because there's something I didn't get, that didn't permit me to have a complete picture of the case. You know better than anyone: They say that one only has a case when he's found the culprits; but it's not true. Just as important as knowing what person or persons are responsible, is knowing the motives. And when Commissioner Flores mentioned these circumstances, I immediately confirmed a suspicion that I hadn't been able to stand up: That Mauricia didn't do this alone, there's someone behind her, and whoever it is has to be a lover, some man that, God alone knows for what reasons, encouraged her to commit the said crime. But all this is just half the story. Now, who this man is, what type of relationship he has with her, has to be ascertained, and, in some way, we have to establish if he had a personal interest in Bartolo García disappearing from the scene. I'm calling you, your honour, conscious of the fact that, since just over 24 hours ago, the accused have been in your hands, so that you can decide what we do. You already know this, but if you want we could soften them up for you, you only have to ask. I'm saying all this so things can be simpler and we don't lose time with any messing about.

Guided by his instincts, the judge decided at this point to interrupt the discussion with Colonel Arriola.

"No, please, don't be upset. I thank you from the bottom of my heart, as you well know, but now that the news has already reached the public it will be better if we follow the judicial procedures as loyally and appropriately as possible. The way to proceed, given the circumstances of this conversation, is for me to dispatch you a backdated order so as not to cause any confusion and for you to put the accused Mauricia Hernández at my disposal in this office as soon as possible. How does that seem?"

The colonel, who, with this, added one more deception to the secret list he was compiling against the 'bureaucrats in ties', as they were called in intimate and confidential circles, reluctantly accepted the decision of Judge Cáceres, and said, don't worry, when the order arrives I'll go to the female prison myself and bring you that woman this very day.

Thus it was. In mid-afternoon, when he had already finished his work, Secretary Schlesinger spotted the colonel's black Ford through the window. He warned everyone, and the officials of the Fourth Court crowded around to take a look at Mauricia.[8] She walked calmly, almost arrogantly it could be said, with her hands tied in front of her and wearing her same old, shabby and crumpled clothes. Colonel Arriola steered her by the arm and carried his hat in his hand. As they entered, the staff almost formed a barrier, straining to see at close quarters the woman about whom, in those days, every member of peaceable and judicious society in Guatemala was talking.

A promise fulfilled, your honour, said the colonel by way of a greeting. Judge Cáceres knew only too well that the colonel did not feel good in the courthouse. The colonel considered it foreign territory, he thought. However, there he was, just as he had promised. In that moment the issue was not the rivalry between the policemen and the lawyers, but the carrying out of an efficient interrogation that would bear fruit. The judge, secretary and officers had great hopes for this particular opportunity. There was Mauricia, they said, now taking stock of her deep philosophical apprehensions. If it were true that something was going on with that mysterious single man who lived on a corner, she would have no motive to hide her

From the Darkness

relationship with him. Moreover, if necessary, and in the pursuit of truth and the common good, the judge was prepared to lie to her, to make her believe that they knew, they had evidence about her relationship with him and consequently it was better for her to confess, because if she did not it would be much worse for her.

This time, the chief officer, the senior pupil, wanted the privilege of helping the judge in the interrogation for himself. By the time that Mauricia and the colonel had sat down, the official was already typing on his machine.

The judge looked at him with an incredulous expression and said:

"And you, are you paying attention to what you're writing? Stop looking at the accused and pay attention to what you're doing."

The chief officer was not the only one watching Mauricia enter by herself, as ever surrounded by men. Everyone had arrived in the hope of seeing her with their own eyes and passing their own judgements. But for days now Mauricia had not been looking ahead of her, had lowered her eyes and was mumbling her replies.

"Don't worry, your honour," the chief officer answered after a moment, "I know this by heart. What's more, as far as her particulars are concerned there's now no need to repeat everything because it is, as we say among ourselves, 'general knowledge'."

"Fine then, proceed with the caution."

The official stood up, adjusted his jacket, gently smoothing down his lapels, became serious and, looking Mauricia in the eye, said in a raised voice:

"Do you swear to tell the truth and nothing but the truth in this interrogation?"

"Yes, I swear," she answered.

"You can sit down," the judge said to both of them, gesturing with his left hand in a relaxed way. "Okay, let me explain," he added, looking at Mauricia. "We've sent for you because we want to expand on your statement. I'm not going to say how, but we've become aware here of certain little things that, if true, can perhaps help your cause. Are you listening to me?"

Mauricia nodded without taking her eyes off her hands as she rested them on the skirt she was wearing.

"Okay, tell us if at the time of Bartolo García's death you were having an affair with another man."

Mauricia felt the question like a rape, like a violent penetration of her private life. No-one even breathed during the long seconds that transpired while, slowly, Mauricia lifted her eyes and looked, one by one, at the expectant faces of all those men who were waiting, who feared her response as if they were hearing their own wives confessing their infidelities. She then regained her strength, her inner security, because she knew that although they were able to judge her, lock her up, even execute her, they feared, dreaded her, because she had transgressed all the boundaries, all the limits within which the peaceful lives of respectable people took place.

"Yes, at that time I was having relations with another man."

"Who was it? Can you tell us his name?"

"He is called Hilario Almeda Godoy," she said, again looking around her.

The judge adjusted himself in his chair and cleared his throat before asking:

"Since when had you been the lover of Hilario Almeda?"

"More or less a month before Bartolo died."

"Be more specific, detail your statements."

"The thing is, at the beginning, Hilario didn't want to touch me. It was little by little. Perhaps he was frightened of Bartolo; but by about the third week of February we began to have a relationship in earnest."

"What does that mean?" asked the judge, satisfying the prurience within the room.

"That on those dates I began to sleep with him."

The judge turned to look at his subordinates with a smile that said 'this is getting good'.

"Let's see," he continued "from what I'm hearing, you have a good memory. Why don't you tell us about this relationship in more detail? For example, how did you know each other, how many times did you have carnal relations, where, if Bartolo ever suspected, etcetera."

A general murmur could be heard that dissipated little by little

From the Darkness

until Mauricia was left with all eyes on her and in the midst of silence.

"We knew each other from years ago. He'd been a friend of Bartolo's all his life. He came to the house and they talked about work. But a few months ago I realised that he was looking at me in another way. Then we began to talk more. He arrived early and, while Bartolo took his time to show up, we talked, about what I don't remember. But at the start of the year, I now not only saw him when he came to the house. He began to spy on me in the street, waiting for me on the way to the market and accompanying me. Finally, he made up his mind to invite me to his house. I didn't dare say no, although I knew what his intentions were. But he only talked to me, he told me he liked me, that he felt very good when he was with me, that he envied Bartolo very much for having me to himself in the house all the time. I told him Bartolo didn't matter, that I only served as his fancy woman. And he said Bartolo was stupid, that if he had me he would care for me a great deal and would always be with me."

"But these are just words," said the judge, anxiously. "How did they translate into actions?"

"I already told you, it was a little later when we began to be intimate and stayed alone in his house whole mornings."

"How many times did you have carnal relations and where? Do you remember?"

"It was six times. All of them in his house in Cantón San Lorenzo."

After her direct reply, the judge stayed quiet for a moment. He was thinking that if a couple have clandestine relations six times in less than thirty days it is because a proximity and very significant intimacy has developed. The way was levelling out for him to be able to ask the questions that were really important in the context of the judicial investigation.

Mauricia, meanwhile, had lowered her eyes. She was thinking that these authoritarian men could not know anything about what it had meant to her, about where a woman is capable of going when she surrenders herself to her instincts. Now not listening to what was being said around her, she remembered how, within an instant, she had been left alone that moment she had curled up into a ball beside Hilario, she remembered how the pain had passed, slowly, and the silence that had descended after the fireworks from the church had thundered in the sky.

"What I'm going to ask you is very important," Judge Cáceres said unexpectedly. "Remember, you are under oath. And remember also that since your arrest you've been in judicial custody. You have nothing to fear. Tell us if Mr Hilario Almeda had knowledge that you were going to poison Bartolo García."

"No," she said, after a moment's doubt, "at no point did I mention it to him. I don't know why, when we were together we never spoke about Bartolo."

"And after the crime? Did you talk to Hilario Almeda and make him aware in any way of what you had done? In other words," added the judge, correcting himself and remembering who he was talking to, "did you share your secret with him?"

"No, I didn't tell him anything, because after Bartolo's death I didn't see him again."

The judge sat up brusquely, perched himself on the edge of his chair, stared Mauricia in the face, and asked:

"Tell me categorically what was your motive for putting poisonous larvae in the water of your common-law husband's gourd?"

Mauricia was taken aback, surprised by the judge's unexpected violence. What was more, it was the first time, as far as she could remember, that instead of calling Bartolo her husband he had called him her "common-law husband".

"I already told you the last time," she said. "It was because he was giving me a bad life. He hit me, and a short while before he had hit me very hard on the arm with a stick, and that was very unfair."

From his experience, the judge knew that the interrogation had reached its conclusion. They were not going to get any more out of Mauricia this time round. It was already enough that she had confessed, with the luxury of detail, about her relationship with Almeda Godoy. Now, all that remained was to follow the thread of this new discovery to its ultimate consequences.

From the Darkness

Wednesday the 12th of April was an important day. The calm tranquillity of the family breakfast of all educated, well-born Guatemalans, duly informed by the serious, responsible and 'impartial' press, was shattered by a scandalous front page headline:

WHOLE FAMILY KILLS HEAD OF HOUSEHOLD
USING GOURD FILLED WITH POISON AND LARVAE.
INNOCENT ACCUSED

The main photograph on the front page showed a wide image of the four accused standing in a line against a wall. Judge Cáceres, already in his office, spread the newspaper out on his desk in order to see the photos better and to read the story in detail. It was an extensive, in-depth article that went from page one to number two, first column. There were one or two errors of precision but, in general, it was a good piece of journalistic investigation. On finishing, the judge turned back to the front page to look at the photo of the accused. He again went over their facial expressions, their clothes, he studied the demeanour of each one, and recalled vividly his own experience of them. There was no doubt that the photo had been taken several hours before they had been interrogated by Judge Portillo, one by one, on the ninth.

But at that moment what the judge was worried about was not that the case had finally been exposed to public opinion. Rather, he was losing sleep about his growing awareness that the more he found out, the less he knew. Now someone else was involved, Mauricia's lover. There was no alternative – he had to investigate this lead in depth. That solitary man, older than Bartolo, whom everyone knew and distrusted, could have been the hidden brains behind the crime.

In an effort to clarify the facts completely and so hand over to the prosecutor a case that did not cause him any headaches and only requiring routine proceedings for sentence to be passed, he had decided to dedicate the rest of the week to clarifying, once and for all, Hilario Almeda's part in the crime against Bartolo. So, that very morning he arranged to summon for interrogation not just Hilario

Oswaldo Salazar

himself, but both of those who were capable of confirming or refuting his statements.

The following day, Thursday the 13th of April, Judge Cáceres received the telegram that announced, with just a few hours of anticipation, Hilario's arrival:

Telegram to Fourth Judge of First Instance
6svm.16dh D.12h R13h35mjed.
Amatitlán, 13 April 1939

Hilario Almeda and Rancho Grande Administrator remain ready to be presented at your office, as rapidly as possible.

A. Fuentes Novella
Justice of the Peace

On the same day, Hilario Almeda Godoy, by now at the office, stated being 55 years of age, a widower, a native and resident of Amatitlán and, in answer to the questions he was asked, declared:

Of course I knew the person who, when alive, was Bartolo García Morán, a great lifetime friend, and also his family. I don't know, therefore, where these false, entirely false, accusations that I was Mauricia's lover come from. How could I betray Bartolo's friendship, on the one hand smiling to him, while on the other screwing his wife? No, your honour, I never had any amorous relationship with the accused. And with respect to whether I knew about the kind of life they were leading, see here, I am not accustomed to meddling in other people's lives, especially if they are my friends. We knew each other from afar, and did not go beyond saying hello, talking when the occasion allowed and, of course, lending each other a hand when required. But it never interested me to know what type of life he gave his wife and children. That's how it was, and what I am going to tell you proves what I have just said is true, I was such a good friend of the family that on the very day Bartolo died they came calling on me to help

From the Darkness

dress the corpse and sort out the ups and downs of the burial. But when I arrived at the house, still not having got over the news, I encountered Bartolo's sister now saying no, many thanks, but the body was still in the hospital awaiting an autopsy and that they had taken the clothing there.

Judge Cáceres stopped the interrogation at this point and, now off the record, asked the declarant if he was prepared to undertake a judicial confrontation with Mauricia. Surprised, but immediately taking control of the situation, Hilario answered yes, the sooner the better. They then brought Mauricia to the office. Because she was already known to the court, she went straight on to respond to the judge's questions.

Secretary Schlesinger brought one more chair to the front of the judge's desk and there the two declarants sat. "What we are going to do," the judge explained to them animatedly, "is called a 'confrontation' and it has as its objective clarifying a situation in which two declarants have contrary opinions. In this case, as you know, the judicial authority wants to know whether you did or did not have carnal relations when Bartolo García Morán was still alive."

"That's the truth," she said in a low voice, without turning to look at Hilario. "As I already told you, it was six times, in his house."

"False!" said Hilario immediately, looking repeatedly at Mauricia and the judge. "That's not true, I've never touched this woman in my life. What's more, if you want to get right to the bottom of this situation, your honour, why don't you question Alberto Aquino Morán, Bartolo's cousin? He told me that she was making love to her future son-in-law, Pedro García. Don't bring me into all this nonsense. I'm far too old to be dragged into this kind of palaver."

Judge Cáceres raised his hand to signal that he should quieten down and asked them if they wanted to talk in private to reach agreement. The law, he said, prohibits the declarants from engaging in a dialogue and reaching agreement in the course of the procedure itself.

They assented and, seeking privacy, walked to the end of the room, beside the window. There they spoke animatedly for ten minutes, then returned to the judge's desk, he with a tranquil expression and she, one of resignation, and both declared that, no, Hilario was right in affirming that they had never had carnal relations.

On feeling the contact of a policeman's hand, Mauricia got up and, without saying goodbye, left in silence by the office door.

On the subsequent two days, Friday the 14th and Saturday the 15th, three witnesses were going to be called to make statements: Alberto Aquino, whom Hilario himself had suggested, Pedro García, for having been alluded to, and Félix Hernández, as a third source of corroboration according to the judge.

Alberto Aquino Morán, who stated he was 52 years of age, married, a native and resident of Amatitlán, declared that yes, just like the rest of the town (these were his words), he knew from hearsay that Mauricia Hernández Urbina was the author of the crime, but that Hilario Almeda was lying when he said it was from his mouth he had heard the rumour she was sleeping with her son-in-law Pedro García. At this point, the judge said thank you and sent him packing. I'm not going to let this one come out with more gossip and complicate the story, he told Secretary Schlesinger. We've enough of that already.

The following day, on the sunny morning of Saturday the 15th of April, Pedro García and Félix Hernández arrived at the office within the same hour.

The former stated that, yes, all the time he had been Rogelia's boyfriend he had seen Hilario Almeda coming to the house. And he remembered perfectly that, after Don Bartolo's death, she, Mauricia, had called on him to sort out the deeds to the property.

When questioned about the same themes, Félix, who had not heard the questions put to Pedro and his replies because he had remained outside, stated that Don Hilario was a friend of the family and came over all the time, and that once his father was dead he had again seen him in the house because, according to what he had found out later, he was going to arrange things with an attorney whose name he didn't remember, things, I mean, he said, to do with the land and house.

From the Darkness

The judge stopped the interrogation there and asked the police officers to return Félix to Number One Barracks. Then he turned to look at the secretary and his officials. No-one said anything. But all were looking at each other with puzzled expressions.

From the Darkness

VIII

The team at the Fourth Court dedicated the following days to discussing names and making the respective consultations with the aim of appointing defence attorneys as soon as possible. The official documentation revealed the names of brilliant young professionals who had accepted the challenge of defending the indefensible: A group of confessed criminals.

On the 20th, they named the attorneys Carlos Martínez Oliva to defend Félix and Federico Barillas Calzia to take up the cause of Pedro García Gesenäuer. Finally, on the 21st, at the explicit request of Mauricia, Rogelia and her guardian Mr Domingo Samayoa Rueda, the attorney Vicente Díaz Samayoa was named to represent both women.

The appointment of Attorney Díaz Samayoa caused particular surprise, above all in Amatitlán's influential circles, for it involved not only an Amatitlánecan by birth, but also because he was the last Gálvez Prize winner and would enjoy the prestige of a trial by combat that promised to hit the front pages. I accepted, he told Jorge, the local journalist, to get to the bottom of this matter and ensure justice is given its due. All I have on my conscience is that, in some way, I am usurping the place of some colleague more qualified than I. Without having to dig very deep, he explained, I have found out that, before being consulted personally by his honour, other colleagues and friends were called, great minds on the Guatemalan bar who, for obvious reasons, I cannot name. But they declined the offer, some for personal reasons and others professional. So, for good or ill, here am I facing this case, perhaps the most sensational in the last few years.

But during these same few days before the naming of the defence attorneys, Judge Cáceres and his loyal confidant, Secretary Schlesinger, saw the case slipping from their hands without being able to do anything about it.

The aforementioned statement amplifications and the new declarants of the 14th of April had only confirmed the confessed guilt of the four accused. But with the intention of getting right to the bottom of the crime's motives, on that same 14th the judge had also called Mauricia and Rogelia to ask for information about the money that Bartolo kept in the house and the way in which he had treated them, as common-law wife and as daughter. Mauricia was not surprised. With great confidence, she told the judge that she had no reason to ask Bartolo for money, since each had their own. And, regarding his, she had taken just one hundred quetzales for the funeral costs, nine days of mourning and candles – and the rest (if they wanted they could go and confirm this) could still be found in the house at the bottom of the chest.

When it fell to Rogelia to answer the question about the (mis)treatment of her father towards her, she took the opportunity to get things off her chest. Visibly perturbed, she said that he hit her a lot, that once when she was sick and her mother insisted on taking her to hospital, he had said "what fucking nonsense", leave her here without doing anything because it would be better if she died. She added that he also whipped Félix, who had the scars to prove it. By way of finishing, she admitted that many times she and her mother had contemplated the possibility of going to live somewhere else but Mauricia had never dared to do so because she was frightened of him.

These statements still did not pose problems for the coherent and complete picture that Judge Cáceres had built up. There were no contradictions. On the contrary, they confirmed fully the thesis of a crime of passion, the classic form of a murder as a last resort to escape a private hell. This, said the judge to the secretary in

From the Darkness

a didactic tone, will be the basis of the defence, mark my words.

But things changed drastically on the 18th of April, when the judge had again summoned Rogelia to expand on her statement in order to clarify the degree of premeditation and she, surprisingly, had said no, now that she thought about it, she had to say that neither she, nor her mother, nor her betrothed and much less her little brother had planned anything. I think, rather, she said, that he committed suicide. Secretary Schlesinger, the official on duty and Judge Cáceres turned to look at each other, frozen for a instant. It's the truth, she continued to say before those incredulous eyes, one day before his death he was speaking with a person, don't ask me if it was a woman or a man because I wouldn't know what to tell you, and I remember that he told them he wanted to die because he was suffering so much. There's more, she added, that day, the 14th, I found out he had been to the pharmacy to buy some tablets.

When the guard had left through the door of the court with the accused on his arm as if in a nuptial procession, Judge Cáceres collapsed with all his weight into the chair in his office. Whore! this man, who rarely uttered bad words, said to his secretary in a tone of despair. What's happening to these people? So this woman comes in, calmly, as if nothing was going on, to refute with an absurd, inconsistent story, everything she had previously confessed in minute detail. Perhaps she doesn't know it but that's just how they sink even deeper. This is going to cause a chain reaction. Now all of them are going to come and tell us lies to acquit themselves. Want proof of what I'm predicting? Summon Pedro García and don't be surprised when he unleashes his new story.

Exactly as he had said, on the 19th Pedro García Gesenäuer, now well-known, was brought in and answered the judge's questions emphasising that all he knew was that Hilario Almeda was a friend of the family, that he knew nothing about the supposed intimate relationship, that no, how could it be, he had never had anything to do with his future mother-in-law, that the entire relationship between them could be reduced to the fact that it was he who obtained for her the insecticide, but that he had never found out what she wanted it for. I just passed it to her on the night of the

Oswaldo Salazar

14th of March; but, as ever, I was coming to see Rogelia. So after giving it to her I forgot about it and did not comment to Rogelia about it at any stage.

"I told you so," the judge said to his secretary, by now aghast at how experienced his boss was. "Now everything's turned into a joke. Well, there's one advantage. If this case is hiding something we have not discovered, this is the only way of getting to know about it. When a group of accomplices abandon their initial judicial declaration and begin to distort things in favour of their individual causes, a mountain of little things come to light. They begin to make mutual accusations in a spiral without end. So the key is to know how to observe and discern with care what's true and what's false, who's who, and what blame lies with each. Now you'll see, this is going to get good. This is no more than the beginning of a long road. I wanted the trial to be quick, like a summary judgement – now we can see it's not going to be like that. The defence lawyers, as young as they are, are going to get stuck in. Let's leave them the most detailed possible inventory of our proceedings. That's the only thing that'll be in our favour when the time comes to pass sentence."

The Fourth Court of First Instance had completed its investigatory work. With the trial now underway, further investigations would depend on the requests of the conflicting parties.

The prosecutor, Attorney J.A. Martínez Perales, the Attorney General of the Nation and head of the justice ministry, was the first to present a brief, dated the 8th of May. In it, he requested four things: first, for a day to be set for the case to be heard; second, for sentence to be passed as soon as possible; third, for the accused in question to be found guilty; and fourth, for capital punishment to be imposed without further delay.

The prosecutor's drastic petition set a precedent. It not only made clear his judicial reading of the case, it also revealed, there at the silent heart of things, the Guatemalan dictatorship's political will – to impart justice without any kind of contemplation or consideration.

Guatemalan society debated its indignation at the crime and the grotesque idea that a woman had to be shot. In those days, for as

From the Darkness

long as could be remembered, a reprieve had always been conceded to women who had committed serious crimes. Generalissimo Jorge Ubico had imposed some exemplary punishments but here he was presented with a golden opportunity to make clear what some people, perhaps, still refused to accept. Order, discipline and, above all, the uncompromising morality of his government, had to be preserved at all costs.

And so began the long, two-year journey during which lawyers, judges, magistrates and military authorities from penitentiary centres exhausted each and every one of the mechanisms foreseen in law for clarifying the facts about the death of Bartolo García Morán. There were two basic strands: on the one hand, the confession made in the first judicial interrogation and, on the other, the radical position adopted by the justice ministry of requesting the maximum penalty for the authors of the crime, and its equivalent for the accomplices.

From then on, the three defence lawyers and the Fourth Court of First Instance articulated this tale through four voices, some of them, at times, out of tune with the sober, formal framework of juridical language.

The memorable brief of Carlos Martínez Oliva, for example, dated the 8th of August, requested:

... that a visual inspection is carried out because the confession is dubious and incongruent.

And with all the rigour that the profound seriousness of the case demanded, yet the supposedly irresponsible way it had been conducted, Attorney Martínez Oliva demanded:

... that plans are drawn up and photos taken of all the details, that the interrogations of all the accused are expanded upon, in order to determine the truth and affirm the congruence or incongruence of the previous statements.

This had to be done, the jurist argued, because the real truth is one thing and flights of the imagination are another very distinct thing; in other words, one thing is the truth established by juridical science and its methods, and another, very different one, the fantastic lies that can be found in literature:

Oswaldo Salazar

It will not escape the learned and prudent approach of His Honour the Judge that, within NOVELS themselves, there are reliable historical sources; but it is very natural and even common that there is also PURE IMAGINATION, and the narrative of these current proceedings could, dangerously, result in one or the other. It falls, then, both to the ministry of justice as well as the defence entrusted to me, to seek truths on which an objective study or juridical analysis of the facts and their relationship with the people being processed can rest.

Carlos Martínez Oliva was the oldest of the defending lawyers and, in a sense, the doyen of the group. His briefs and allegations were always tinged with passion, by an imposing and deliberately dramatic language. But, that aside, it was he who set a precedent.

For his part, the young, recently graduated Vicente Díaz Samayoa, more restrained and orderly, waited for Attorney Martínez Oliva to establish the guidelines and, in general, produced a balanced, prudent, measured brief appealing to the judge's conscience solely through the means of rational argument.

Finally, Federico Barillas Calzia, the last to pronounce on each of the petitions, characterised his defence by limiting himself strictly to the interests of Pedro García, his client.

In the brief of the 8th of August, Attorney Martínez Oliva had sowed doubt about whether there was a plot. It was quite apparent that, perhaps in pursuit of notoriety on the Guatemalan bar, the defender had gone far beyond limiting himself to a simple defence of Félix. His briefs spoke of all the accused, of a general situation which he saw as corrupted, perverted by concealed interests. The denunciation of an alleged manipulation of the facts carried with it the grave accusation of a perversion of justice. However, in spite of the denunciation contained in his brief, at least in the following two months, the matter went no further.

Between August and the end of October 1939, the only events were:

August 18th: Mauricia, in an amplification of her interrogatory statement, retracted her initial confession absolutely.

From the Darkness

August 21st: When the carriage driver, Miguel Ángel Suárez Ponciano, was questioned, he declared that on the 15th of March of that year, Rogelia Hernández García had told him it was necessary to take her father to the hospital.

August 24th: The declarant Félix Hernández, when asked repeatedly whether he had spoken with anyone nearby about the fact that his father would be poisoned, answered that, beforehand, he had spoken with no-one; but that, afterwards, Pedro Quezada's mother had told him he shouldn't say it had been Pedro who had poisoned his father but that it had been his own mother, Mauricia Hernández Urbina.

August 29th: The accused Pedro García Gesenäuer admitted that on the day Bartolo García Morán died he had changed jobs: from the El Rancho Grande farm to the Los Cuchales farm owned by Don Abraham Gálvez, arguing that the reason for this was that the latter was going to pay him more.

The month of October passed uneventfully. All the action in the case developed in the private chambers of the defence lawyers. There they prepared the pleas prior to the Fourth Court's sentence. As was to be expected, the first and most emotive juridical argument was rendered on the 6th of November by Carlos Martínez Oliva. In it he requested basically that in the name of his defendant a new COMPREHENSIVE INVESTIGATION be undertaken with the aim, in his own words, of clarifying the facts.

As in any judicial 'plea', the first part was a synthesis of the development of the proceedings since the police dispatches, the opening of the case, the interrogations and the furnishing of evidence. It constructed a sketch, very often a caricature, of how the process would appear when the judge summed up in passing sentence. In it, he was seeking to bring together all the material of interest to the defence.

In his synthesis of the facts, Attorney Martínez Oliva returned to his arguments from the 8th of August according to which there had, throughout the proceedings, been a dark manipulation of the facts with hidden intentions. It read:

Oswaldo Salazar

Next thing, strangely, Mauricia Hernández Urbina and her daughter Rogelia Hernández García ended up being detained, and in storybook fashion they were made to relate a police chronicle to a judge completely unaware of the proceedings thus far and outside his legal jurisdiction. To make matters worse, in it the accusation against Pedro Quezada was ditched and the family was accused of complicity in a deed that should have been investigated in a much more intelligent way.

With all the convenience and mendacious mania of NOVEL-WRITING, all that this has succeeded in doing is bringing about this trial and, around it, giving great publicity to this crime in the tabloids, thus making it appear terrifying in order to justify, before opinion that is so badly described as public, the position that it requires an exemplary punishment because of how it mocks society in general.

What is the result of this fictitious mess? Nothing more and nothing less than the fact that it has not been able to establish what, forgive the tautology, really happened in reality. It is sufficient, by our scientific and as such fully objective conjecture, to state that what appears here in these proceedings and is being thrown at the family of Mr García Morán is 'A PRODUCT OF THE IMAGINATION' and that the proceedings HAVE NOT BEEN APPROPRIATELY PURIFIED – have not been distilled in the laboratories of juridical science – because of a flight of malice from feverish minds wanting to use the power at their disposal to introduce lies, and not what they should be using it for.

The entire PENNY DREADFUL that has been formulated with a manifest and pathetic lack of grace and intelligence is as of nothing in the face of the certain and unquestionable strength of the argument that follows: If Mauricia Hernández Urbina filled the gourd and added toxins to it with the intention of poisoning Bartolo García Morán with the premeditated aim of appropriating what he had at his disposal or of removing him because he was giving her a bad life, why was she the first to ask for help to save the life of her own supposed victim?

And, later, why seek the means to DENOUNCE the existence of a

From the Darkness

poisoning (crime) knowing, supposedly, that it was she who was guilty (so it is imagined)? And, moreover, to make this allegation to the doctor at the hospital, when she could avoid doing so by giving an account of a death whose cause had been innocent and not imputable. Undoing these arguments is a useless and inconclusive task; but comfort, laziness, is unjust and carries with it very serious issues of conscience that are of great significance to judicial life. It is public knowledge that novelists have no qualms about characterising dirty lies as pristine truths.

To conclude, I only want to bring up one more matter of opprobrium: it is evident from the writs (pages 60 and 61 of the 2nd Part called 'Evidence') that Félix indicated that Miguel Peralta and Marcelo Palencia had seen and could confirm something, and this appears to be something which could be insignificant or could be the solution to the juridico-moral problem that we the prosecution, the defence and His Worship the Judge are facing; but this has not been clarified, because the NOVEL is now complete and so it has to be thus.

In this plea, probably the most disturbing part of the whole trial, three essential facts to which there were no definitive responses throughout the evidence and the reflections of each side were denounced.

First, it denounced the unexplained fact as to why, with proceedings in the Fourth Court of First Instance into the murder of Bartolo García Morán already underway, the confessed culprits were sent to the Fifth Court of First Instance that had no jurisdiction and was unaware of the process already initiated in the other court.[9]

Second, it denounced the investigation as being incomplete and unsatisfactory as long as it did not address why the same supposed murderess sought medical help and, later, took the trouble to make a legal denunciation to a competent authority.

And third, it denounced the fact that, despite expanding on his statements, the accused Félix Hernández García identified (with first names and surnames) two witnesses who saw and were sure about "something" that could be the solution to the problem, yet the Fourth Judge never called the said persons to make a statement.[10]

These questions were met with a long silence until, on the seventh of December, the Day of the Bonfire of the Devil, Vicente Díaz Samayoa delivered the final version of his plea to the Fourth Court. Faithful to the formal habit of synthesising the case, it read as an ordered recollection of the proceedings followed by a display of motives in which the young professional, as subtle as he was in everything he did, especially that which he edited, hinted that the confession of the first judicial investigation, albeit valid, revealed evidence of the doubtful attitude of the accused about attributing to themselves full responsibility for the crime 'unreservedly'. In other words, Attorney Díaz Samayoa was questioning the real 'value' of the confession and finished off by requesting that, under the circumstances, in the case of the defendant Rogelia Hernández García only the offence of covering up but not that of authorship of the crime be imputed.

Deep down, both Martínez Oliva and Díaz Samayoa were in agreement. The first confession, the evidential basis for the justice ministry's petition seeking the maximum punishment, was not totally valid. While the first denounced manipulation and errors in the judicial procedures, the second only requested the judicious consideration of a confession that could not be taken at face value.

Finally, on the 12th of January 1940, Federico Barillas Calzia, in his defence of Pedro García Gesenäuer, limited himself to signalling that, taking into account the complete sequence of statements and extended statements by his client and others, it could only be concluded that the accused had been an accomplice but not the author of the crime against Bartolo García Morán. Taking the opposite position to Martínez Oliva, Barillas Calzia accepted fully the validity of the proceedings in both their content and formal mechanisms, and only asked that, in the face of doubt, inconsistencies and contradictory testimony, the sentence pronounced against Pedro García, his defendant, be the minimum.

With this plea, the minimal requirements for the judge to pass sentence were finally completed. Under normal circumstances,[11] sufficient investigations had been conducted for a quick sentence to follow on naturally within a short period. However, the sensational, lurid and unusual nature of the case meant that two months later, on the 7th of March, the Fourth Judge (still Attorney Cáceres) would take a new direction in the investigation. Unexpectedly, he resolved to order an investigation into Mauricia Hernández Urbina's previous life and to determine if the larvae used were poisonous or not.[12]

This concession by the judge, obviously a response to the arguments of Attorney Martínez Oliva, did not throw up satisfactory results in the following months. The new justice of the peace in Amatitlán questioned neighbours and friends of the couple with the aim of establishing what kind of life they had led in the past. Nothing was ascertained that was not already known previously: that Bartolo had met Mauricia as a maid in his house when his first wife, Doña Lucía, had been alive; that he had had a son by this first marriage, Lencho, who had died approximately ten years before; and that Mauricia was an isolated person, with few friends, who never became close to anyone in particular.

Repeatedly, Secretary Schlesinger expressed to the judge, now Gonzalo Menéndez de la Riva, his growing conviction that the formal nature of the judicial interrogations inhibited the spontaneity of the witnesses. One thing, he told him, is what everyone says outside the court and another completely different thing is what they come and say here, as if one were dealing with completely different people. There should be some mechanism that gave sufficient confidence to witnesses to come and say what they really know or what their intuition tells them. Don't say that out loud, Judge Menéndez de la Riva answered, because our police friends will say that only their methods are effective. We do what we can with the little that we have. The truth will come out when we least expect it.

The judge's blind confidence in a justice blinder still was not going to yield much fruit on this occasion. Five months passed between the decision to return to the investigation and the day on which the Fourth Court of First Instance delivered its sentence. During that time, nothing significant came to light. The only thing with any novelty that was added was a small collection of letters that Rogelia Hernández made available for her defence. There were four original letters written by Pedro García Gesenäuer. Three of them addressed to her father ('Mr Don Bartolo García, For your attention'), and the other to her ('My beautiful girl'), as his betrothed.

Attorney Díaz Samayoa, on submitting these into the trial, had commented that they were being handed over as proof of the intimate relationship that Pedro García had with the family and, also to dispel any doubt about the great esteem in which Pedro had held the deceased. Moreover, the lawyer added, they contained evidence of Pedro's debt to Bartolo García.

In reality, if the small collection was proof of anything, it was of how impossible the accused Pedro García Gesenäuer found it to express himself in writing and of how, in his immediate past, there had been a mystery that had not been aired in the trial until that moment. But the letters' syntactic distortion was so great that it made them practically illegible.[13]

During these months the case totally disappeared from the public mind. Only those involved were waiting upon the pending decisions. The defence lawyers, fearful of taking any extreme steps, decided to wait patiently for the day on which the new Fourth Judge would deliver his sentence.

That day arrived. It was on the morning of the 10th of August of 1940. The long historical account with which the sentence opened left no loose ends. Little by little, as the tale advanced towards its resolute conclusion, the enormous influence that the defence arguments had exercised on Judge Menéndez de la Riva could be noted. Passing through the typical sub-divisions of sentences as they were delivered – AS A RESULT, CONSIDERING AND THEREFORE – the document concluded that Pedro Francisco García Gesenäuer and Mauricia Hernández Urbina, authors of the crime of murder,

... receive the incommutable penalty of 15 years in Correctional Prison that, taking account of the time already served, the former must serve in the Central Penitentiary and, the latter, the Women's

From the Darkness

Prison; that Félix and Rogelia Hernández García are accomplices in the same crime for which the incommutable sentence of six years and eight months is imposed on them.

These words did not surprise anyone. The sentences coincided almost exactly with what the lawyers had sought for their defendants. However, some, in spite of their youth, were conscious that they were most probably merely experiencing a fleeting, ephemeral happiness. It was impossible that the prosecutor in the case would not appeal against a ruling that had been so far from his original petition applying for capital punishment for those with proven authorship in the crime. Consequently, foreseeing this eventuality, the defence lawyers decided to appeal against the decision themselves in order to attenuate even further the court's already soft decision.

The case was elevated to the Court of Appeal. It met with the honourable collegiate team of Court Three. More than four months passed before their final decision was known. Thus, on the 28th of January 1941, a decision that based its findings on those issued by the Fourth Court was made public. The Considerants were now disposed towards the drastic position of his honour J. A. Martínez Perales, Attorney General of the Nation. And the "therefore" surprised everyone for the striking about-turn of 180 degrees that it made to the previous sentence. The authors were sentenced to capital punishment and the accomplices to six years and eight months in prison.

Two days later, the 30th of January, the latest Fourth Judge of First Instance, Attorney J.C. Martínez Perales, the Attorney General's brother, was prevented from hearing the case because of this relationship, and passed it on to the Fifth Court of First Instance under the direction and authority of Attorney Eugenio Nuila.

The last resort had been exhausted. After this, all that remained was to await the execution. But a situation that had not come out into the open for two whole years and that not only put in question the courts' investigative effectiveness but, in some ways, revived the original fears of Carlos Martínez Oliva, was yet to be revealed.

On the 23rd of May, by any reckoning well outside the process by which a last effort to appeal had been made and had by now failed, Pedro García, with the evident help of a convict more erudite than he, sent the following missive to the director of the central penitentiary:

Mr Director of this Penal Centre
Your Good Offices

Respectable Sir,
For having to make some revelations of a very serious type and related to my cause, I beg you in a most earnest manner to be so kind as to concede me an audience of a personal nature.

Very gratefully yours for any deference to the above that it would serve to dispense me, I remain respectfully yours, your humble servant,
Pedro F. García G.

Three days later, on the 26th of May, Judge Nuila called the offender García Gesenäuer to make another statement. He did so with reluctance, knowing that nothing, or virtually nothing, could be done at this stage. The chapel of rest, he told his subordinates, opens days before the execution. This poor man must have already entered a hallucinatory process in which, at times, he believes he can remember what never happened, hear what never was said and, of course, see what is not there. But, never mind, we have to grant this petition.

Towards mid-morning, the court constable announced the prisoner's arrival. The judge, like someone forced to drink something bitter, told him he could let him pass and instructed his officials to take a note of the extraordinary statement that Pedro was preparing to give.

"Cheer up, your honour," said the chief officer. "Who knows, perhaps all of a sudden this man is bringing something under his arm that's going to cause an upset in this case?"

From the Darkness

"Perhaps," he responded lazily. "But let me tell you, I doubt it very much."

Pedro appeared in the doorway, tall, thin, serious and with a decisive expression, distinct from his usual submissiveness. The chief officer quickly swore him in and pulled up a chair for him to sit in front of the judge.

"Pedro," said the judge in an admonitory tone, "I hope you're aware that there is very little we can do for you at this point. I allowed you to come because it's my obligation to listen to you until the last moment; but all this has already been through court."

"Yes, Mr Judge; but I need you to hear me out because what I have to tell you is important."

"Let's see," said the judge, reclining on his chair, "what's it about?"

"It's something I've known since all this began, but never dared tell anyone. Not even my attorney. For two years I've kept it secret."

"Well, as I already told you," said the judge, "it's a little late to talk; but go ahead anyway, let's get this over and done with."

Pedro adjusted himself in his chair while fidgeting nervously with his hat.

"It happens that on the 27th of March of 39, nearly two weeks after Don Bartolo's death, I went to the train station there in Amatitlán to see off my dad who was going to Tiquisate to get work. There I was, doing no harm to anyone, when I got a great fright. Someone put their hand on my shoulder. Forcefully, like someone who had just found what they'd being digging around looking for."

The chief officer's fingers flew across the typewriter keyboard. Not one word of that suspenseful story was lost.

"It was," Pedro continued recounting, "Don Emilio Barrera."

"He's the landowner who has already been interrogated as part of these proceedings, right? Or am I wrong?" interrupted the judge, frowning.

"The very same," Pedro assented immediately.

"And then? What the fuck did he want?"

"Well, let me tell you, we talked for a while."

"Do you remember what you talked about?"

"About different things. But that's not what's interesting. What's important was what he said to me at the end. So, without knowing why, he stared at me maliciously and said: 'Have things improved for you with Bartolo's death?'"

"So? What did that mean?" asked the judge, intrigued.

"I wondered the same thing. I didn't know what he was talking about. Sorry, I did know, but I didn't understand what he was referring to with those words that he had just fired off at me like that, without explanation and in a tone of complicity."

"And you," inquired the judge, "what did you say?"

"The truth. That, on the contrary, since that day everything had been going wrong for me, my situation was very bad. Then, as they all are those bosses who don't listen to what you tell them, Don Emilio told me I should rest easy because he could assure me there was no doctor that could discover the insecticide with essence of chiltepe chile and larvae and this was well proven."

"Let's see," said the judge, trying to unravel the tangle, "at that time Mauricia and you had still not confessed. Does this mean that Barrera already knew it had been you and he even knew the details that the police had been guarding with all the confidentiality of the case?"

"Well, yes, that's what I've been thinking for these two years," said Pedro with an air of innocence.

"But how did Barrera know all this? What relationship did he have with both of you?"

"With both of us is a lot of people. With Mauricia, you mean."

"Explain."

"I don't know how far the investigation would've gone, Mr Judge, but many people believed that Don Emilio was Mauricia's lover. Perhaps that's how the boss got to know."

There was a silence that demonstrated that Judge Nuila did not know what to continue asking.

"I'm telling you," continued Pedro, in full control of his words, "because, when he realised I wasn't answering, he put his hand on my shoulder and told me not to worry about Mauricia because he'd already advised her what to do."

From the Darkness

"Advised how? Did he say what he was referring to?"

"Yes, I remember it as if it was yesterday. He told me he'd already given her some of his quetzales and, moreover, he'd already promised her the land for Félix, her son, so he had somewhere to sow."

"Are you suggesting Mauricia murdered her husband at the behest of Emilio Barrera? Tell me, because if not, why did he need to resort to blackmail for her to keep quiet? And if all this is true, what interest did he have in killing Bartolo García? Have you any idea about that?"

"I'm only telling you what I know, what Don Emilio told me at the train station. What's true is that the only thing Don Emilio could envy Bartolo for was his woman. Maybe he did it so he could be left with her."

"Did he tell you anything else?" the judge asked.

"Yes, he added that in the remote possibility of them taking us prisoner we wouldn't be in the can for long because he'd give us everything we needed to get out and he'd pay for the attorneys. But it was really true, believe me, that it was not going to be for me but he wanted Mauricia to be free."

"Anything else?"

"Only, in order to corroborate my story, that later we went to have some drinks at 'Grace's' and we bought rum in Eugenio Pérez's liquor store."

"Did you tell Mauricia about this unusual episode, to find out what was going on between them?"

"I was confused. What Don Emilio told me scared me. I was only thinking about someone discovering what we'd done. That's why, when I saw her, I told her about the poison, that thing, according to Don Emilio, about there being no doctor who could discover it. But she laughed in my face and told me it was a lie, that where was there not going to be a doctor who could discover it."

"I have to give some thought to all this," said the judge, rubbing his brow, "but, it occurs to me, how did Barrera know you were in danger of being captured? How did he know about your complicity, if at that moment no-one even knew if you had done anything or not? It has to have been someone directly involved."

"Mauricia," retorted Pedro, "it was surely her who told him that I'd taken the remedy."

"Remedy? Don't you mean 'poison'?"

"No, I mean 'remedy', because I never knew that the insecticide was for killing Don Bartolo. She tricked me saying that she needed it to cure her pig."

"Okay, okay, this is flour from another sack. Let's not discuss that now. But, tell me: did you see Barrera again after this encounter at the station?"

"From a distance, in the stubble fields of his sister, Victoria Barrera."

"Is there anyone who can corroborate your statement? Any witnesses to this conversation?"

"No, Mr Judge, I'd be lying if I were to give you a name. And now that I think about it, it was like that because Don Emilio was very careful to ensure nobody was around and to speak to me, all the time, in a lowered voice, in a tone of secrecy."

"Anything else to add?"

"Only one thing," he said, straightening his torso and lifting his head, "whenever and wherever you say so, I'm ready to maintain everything I've told you in the presence of Don Emilio."

Nearly a month after this expansion on Pedro's statement, Judge Nuila sent the mayor of Amatitlán the following note:

Ensure A. Eugenio Pérez (he has a liquor store there) presents himself at this Office, for the undertaking of judicial proceedings, on the coming 23rd or 24th, under caution (urgent).

To which, the following day, the mayor replied:

It is my humble duty to inform you that he who is summoned on the reverse, Mr Eugenio Pérez, is not known in this municipality.[14]

Incredibly, Judge Nuila did not call Emilio Barrera to make a statement. In his place, on the 30th of the same month he called Mauricia Hernández to expand on her previous statements. The

From the Darkness

declarant denied everything, said it was false that Don Emilio would have talked to her in any way, that he was completely ignorant of who poisoned the water of her husband, and how, and that she only had a relationship with Mr Barrera as a landlord, never of another type. She added that it was not true she had a sick pig although, yes, she had one but she sold it to Doña Victoria Figueroa and she could tell you the pig was healthy.

On the 29th of July the same Court Three that had issued its condemnation, incorporated into the body of its judgement the decision by the president relating to a pardon, which in its final section read:

CONSIDERING: that on examination of the proceedings that have been pursued in the particular case there do not appear to be special circumstances deserving of the mercy requested,
THEREFORE: the President of the Republic AGREES: to deny the pardon that has been requested. PLEASE CONVEY THIS.
Ubico.

The Generalissimo's tacit instructions were always: "If you're going to do something, do it in an exemplary way." That meant, in this case, death by firing squad had to have a noble social purpose. Ideally, those condemned to death had to be executed in those communities in which the crime had been committed, so that people would know what to expect if they transgressed the law. Added to that, the diligent attention given by the public servants to what had been said and, above all, what had not been said, in the presidential discourse, meant that the military high command's initial decision was for the offenders to be despatched by force of arms inside Amatitlán cemetery. However, for practical reasons that were not made clear, on the 31st of July (Saint Ignacio's Day) all the orders were changed and it was decided, finally, that the execution would be carried out on the central penitentiary's inner patio.

There was no need to give the case publicity. It had been, without any doubt, the most sensational case in Guatemala, exactly as Judge Portillo had predicted two years before. So this decision had been made bearing that in mind and, on the other hand, it was more effective to do it in the capital because, owing to its profile, the case had touched every level of Guatemalan society. The opportunity to set an example such as this could not be passed over if what they were dealing with here was safeguarding the most basic values – those of the family, the cornerstone of modern society and state. Moreover, the fact that a woman would be shot on the penitentiary's now mythical inner patio gave the deed more symbolic force.

On that same Thursday the 31st of July, Mauricia received three visits. The first was that of the Fifth Court's notifying officer, who took her the news of the sentence. On his way to the cell, the officer was accompanied by the central prison's female director. He handed over the document to a Mauricia who was perplexed, almost incapable of answering, and who, after hearing the routine explanation, remained seated on a bench, distraught, leaning back against the wall with the open paper in her hand, faint and without strength.

Hours later, with all the parsimony and gravity that the case merited and also accompanied by the director and, this time, by several warders, the parish priest of the Church of Saint Sebastián arrived. A supernatural halo surrounded him. The women accompanying him, attentive to his slow walk, to the movement of his ample cassock, to his halting, wise voice, and to the noble gesture of his right hand that blessed anyone who asked, walked in silence, absorbed by he who possessed the divine power to pardon sins, even one as grave as that committed by the condemned. On reaching the door, the Father allowed them to open it but at that moment, with a gesture of apostolic superiority, told them not to worry, that he must be alone with her, that this was his duty. The door closed and the warders remained outside in expectant silence. A few minutes passed and, little by little, they began to hear a growing murmur, his voice emphasising short questions that were impossible to understand clearly, then an immediate reply, more like a growl, an animal grunt, than an articulated phrase. The women guarding the door looked at each other without understanding what was going on inside. They noted quickly that the Father had become exasperated, that he was angry, they heard steps, clothes ruffling, his voice becoming clearer and approaching the door and, at last, they saw

From the Darkness

his figure in the doorway. His face had lost its serenity completely. He crossed the corridor with large strides and his clothing flapped as if he was in the middle of a storm. The women, all eyes at that moment, returned to look at the dark interior of the cell. There was Mauricia seated on the wooden bench, her torso bent across her knees and her face in her hands, crying softly. One of the women, moved by compassion and without thinking, tried to enter to console her; but another, more experienced, grabbed her by the arm and did not let her go in.

The last hours of the morning went by. The door opened again when they brought Mauricia lunch. She had moved to the end of the bench, to the corner of the cell. They found her curled up into a ball, cloaked in her shawl, her eyes open, staring at an indefinite point. The warders knew she would not eat the food, that they would enter later and the meal would be untouched. It was a pure formality. What they did not know was that they would have to open the cell again at the request of an unexpected visitor.

A few minutes before two in the afternoon, César Izaguirre, well known in police circles of the time, made his appearance. The civil servant had with him the latest edition of the famous police newspaper, *La Gaceta de la Policía Nacional*, an organ devoted to divulging the achievements of Ubico's police. He had met briefly with the director of the prison to make her aware that it was of great importance that she permit him a brief interview with the offender Mauricia Hernández Urbina, in order to give the citizenry complete information. "I don't need to explain to you, it is known," he had said to the director, "that we are dealing with a special case, no more nor less than the second woman ever to face the firing squad in Guatemala. This interview will be," he finished, "the icing on the cake for a case that has been carried out in an impeccable way by the national police." Of course, the director had no objection at all to the initiative. She assented, with the proviso that she must be present, to Izaguirre entering the prison and the cell of the woman condemned to death. The interview, according to the rumours of warders and offenders, took place without any surprises, for about 15 minutes.

Oswaldo Salazar

The functionary entered, paper in hand and pen at the ready. When he crossed the threshold of the cell, a headline crossed his mind depicting him arriving at the prison by himself, 'invested with all the authority and dignity that his high office granted him' he thought it would read, as if a third party were there to write up this unusual interview with a dead woman.

Upon leaving, Izaguirre saw two police officers who had not been there when he had entered, standing vigil at the door like the guardians of a tomb.

From the Darkness

Epilogue

It was still dark outside and the first footsteps, the first voices, and the rustling of police officers and warders behind the door could still not be heard. Mauricia, who had stopped crying hours before, remained inert, seated at the bench where she had passed the last few hours. Her mind was filled with a confusion of images with neither order nor arrangement – Félix, Hilario, her carefree childhood, her mother, the reflections on the lake in the afternoon sun... and amidst this silence attended only by her memories she thought of Father Bernabé Salazar, she remembered the day on which the young priest, on a visit to Amatitlán, had given her a stamp of the Just Judge, that little Nazarene Jesus famous as an advocate for lost causes, from the Cathedral in the capital.

Suddenly, at the moment Mauricia raised her gaze to the dark end of the cell, it seemed to her that she was looking at the Father's small, plump figure. There he was, serene, smiling, as if he had simply passed through the walls yet did not have to explain himself. She saw him with half-closed eyes as if he were a visitor from another world. She watched him greet her and walk towards her, kissing the stole he brought in his chubby white hand, reciting incomprehensible Latin formulas and bringing up a chair to sit right in front of her.

I have come to hear your confession, daughter, do you want to tell me your sins? she heard the Father say. Mauricia had lowered her eyes like someone repenting in silence. Now all she saw were the hands of the priest holding a wooden rosary, the shining crucifix swinging to and fro. He, too, had been condemned to death by the justice of men. I understand that you don't want to, that perhaps you cannot speak because of the condition you find yourself in, she heard. I only want to know if you are sorry for all the bad things you have done, woman, tell me as best you can. Sitting there without strength, as if she had a body of rags, empty, inert, she had just enough breath to nod her head.

"*Ego te absolvo a peccatis tuis. In nomine Patris, et Filii, et Spiritus Sancti. Amen,*" she heard, at last, as if these words alone resonated in her head.

There was a moment of deep silence. Suddenly, the world surrounding her appeared to have been converted into the ephemeral, captured scene of an absurd canvas, that snare in time where she had been imprisoned. She knew that Father Bernabé had fulfilled his mission, and this gave her back the peace of mind lost so long ago. When she raised her eyes, the Father was still there, in the centre of the cell, standing. But now it seemed to her that she could no longer speak to him because he would not hear her, he was far away. He was still smiling. And his kindly, compassionate look seemed to be telling her not to be frightened, that in some way everything was now a memory and there was no longer any reason for waiting or anguish.

Then she heard the door opening and, in a reflex, turned to look at it. The prison director, visibly distressed, stopped at the threshold, looking at her without saying anything. The guards and some warders following her entered hurriedly into every corner. Several minutes later, the representatives of the central penitentiary's committee appeared and spoke with the director for a few moments in low, sibilant tones, turning to look inside the cell. Finally, two men entered in silence and proceeded to tie Mauricia's hands. They removed her gently, supporting her by the left arm, and guided her to the vehicle ready outside.[15]

It was not yet five in the morning. The darkness of the night began to dissipate in a cold, tenuous breeze that revealed a sky of grey clouds. It was the first time in many months that Mauricia had

From the Darkness

seen the streets. But now it was completely different. Where were the people? Were these houses reflected in the wet sidewalks inhabited? And if they were sleeping in those warm, protected enclosures, would all the families there be honest, loving and happy? For a moment, watching distractedly as the world went by through the window, Mauricia felt that she had already died, that she was returning to visit and nobody had noticed her presence.

They arrived at the top of 18th Street and there, on the left, sticking out, was the bulk of the penitentiary with its impassable walls and imposing, vigilant towers. The enormous doors remained open and there were two stationary guards on each side. The driver reduced speed and they entered in silence until stopping in front of a group of serious, elegant people waiting beneath wide umbrellas in the fine, almost weightless drizzle. Two guards helped her out of the car and escorted her through the offices, inner patios and remand cells until they reached the central patio in which two leafy trees had been planted at both ends. Mauricia saw at the bottom a large number of men formed into a compact block and remaining silent. At the other end, to her right, the soldiers of the jail who made up the reinforced firing squad were escorting a man in a tie (who was holding some sheets of paper in his hand) and Pedro, whom she had not seen for two years. There he was with his eyes fastened on the ground, with his felt hat and a simple white, long-sleeved shirt buttoned up to his neck.

Secretary Cifuentes accompanied Pedro to where they had halted with Mauricia and proceeded to read out the death sentence issued by the Third Court of the Court of Appeal, as well as the ruling on the annulment and the governmental accord by which they had been denied a reprieve. When he had finished, they were steered to the rear part of the prison's so-called triangle, exactly below the famous *cux* tree.[16] All the authorities who by law should be present for the execution were there.

As his last act before leaving the matter in military hands, the governor asked both prisoners if they wished to be blindfolded. They said yes. Then they were led to the wall and were seated on a bench, recently painted for the occasion. Meanwhile, the commands ordering a formation of two rows of eight pairs could be heard. There were 16 soldiers in total, half standing and the other half kneeling on the ground. They wielded their rifles in accordance with the orders they were being given. Halt! Attention! Ready! Aim!...[17] And the prisoners only heard the metallic noises and the anonymous voices as if dreaming, as if it were not for them.

Mauricia raised her face. She remembered that a second ago, while they were putting the blindfold on, she had seen the *cux* tree to her right. She felt the cool air that brought the smell of that other tree she had climbed as a girl and for a moment, far away from everything, she could see from there, on-high, the mud street leading to her house and, below, the shadow of the thick branches and her brothers playing catch with other children, oblivious to everything, and repeating the same game infinite times.[18]

From the Darkness

Author's narrative elaborations

1. That Wednesday, at least for those working in the fields far from the town centre, was a peaceful, routine day. However, around the lake and the central park, at about mid-morning, there was excited anticipation and a general hubbub. Since the 4th of March the newspaper (in the sports section of *El Imparcial*) had been announcing a cycling race *between the capital and Amatitlán, round trip, exclusively for children up to 16 years of age.*

2. In those days, as far as public opinion was concerned, things were calm and it seemed that nothing unusual was happening. The press headlines followed a traditional formula: News about the European war and the efficiency of Ubico's administration. The front page of *El Imparcial* from this day noted:

HITLER LIQUIDATES THE CZECH STATE
32 MORE HOUSES INAUGURATED IN THE DISTRICT
UBICO IN PRESIDENTIAL HOMAGE

3. In those days, although it might seem strange, telephones were a novelty. Amatitlán, perhaps because of its proximity to the capital, had been among the first towns to have the four indispensable units: those of the police, the post office, the court and the hospital.

4. It came out on page 4 of *El Imparcial* and said:

ON A VISIT TO AMATITLÁN. Political Chief Inspects. Yesterday morning the departmental political chief, General Mauricio Serrano Muñoz, together with his Secretary, Colonel Clodomiro Barillas, carried out an inspection visit in the municipality of Amatitlán.

Oswaldo Salazar

General Serrano saw confirmation of the highway's good condition as well as the touristic works on the banks of the lake, where two new piers are being constructed. The banks, at the part where the booths are, have been cleaned with the aim of leaving the beaches in the best condition for bathers.

In the hospital, extension works are being carried out to construct a new kitchen and lodgings for the use of employees, as well as a water tank.

5. Behind these words had been a long and byzantine discussion, still going on, according to which, for the police, lawyers are all talk, while they, immersed in the heart of the "play", are "men of action".

6. According to the logic of the judicial 'career', the judge was referring to those who would have the privilege of taking charge of a case as sensational as that which they now had in their hands. Moreover, there is a trace of impotence in his words because Attorney Portillo was conscious that it was not he who had control over this.

7. The young pupil lawyer was especially impressed, in those days, by three novels that had been published in the United States: *The Postman Always Rings Twice*, by James M. Cain; *They Shoot Horses, Don't They?*, by Horace McCoy; and *Thieves Like Us*, by Edward Anderson. His comfortable and confident command of English enabled him to read them in the original.

8. In the mind of Secretary Schlesinger, still under the hypnotic influence of James M. Cain's prose and his fearful novel *The Postman Always Rings Twice*, the woman who came walking down the street was a creole epigone of Cora, the sensual and irresistible Cora Papadakis, the criminal lover of Frank Chambers.

9. On the 29th of May, Martínez Oliva had presented a nullity of the judicial proceedings undertaken by the Fifth Judge. His intention, obviously, had been to invalidate a confession that, in his opinion, had been carried out in suspiciously irregular conditions. The brief, in its essential passage, read:

Therefore, I request that it is declared insubstantial that performed by the Fifth Justice of the Peace, for not having jurisdiction (given that his competence covers territory up to the boundary of the Municipality of Guatemala City). And that this insubstantiality should be put forward as an INCIDENTAL PLEA so that a ruling can be made on that performed by the Fifth Justice of the Peace and so contained within the court orders, from folio 45 to 51, that is, those proceedings from the 9th of April to the 10th of the same month and year.

On the 5th of July Judge Cáceres declared the nullity without basis.

10. This "something", marked with the inscription in pencil 'NB' in the margin of page 60 of the 2nd Part, says:

The accused Félix Hernández, for his part, wants to make it known that there are two witnesses who saw Pedro Quezada leave the place where he and his father were working on the day the latter was poisoned and that those witnesses are Miguel Peralta and Marcelo Palencia.

Reviewing the process, it is surprising to verify that these witnesses were not called into what remained of the trial in order for the judge to reach a decision on sentencing. But more surprising still is realising that in spite of the fact that Attorney Martínez Oliva had complained that this had not been investigated in the evidential phase, he himself never asked the judge to call the said witnesses to be interrogated.

11. In this context, more narrative than juridical, it turns out to be impossible as well as undesirable to define with precision what the enigmatic expression 'normal circumstances' means, 'normality' (it seems) being a tightrope suspended between supports of air.

Oswaldo Salazar

12. It is worth saying that this renewed intent at investigation was the last act of Attorney Cáceres as Fourth Judge of First Instance. As seen, he was replaced for some time by Gonzalo Menéndez de la Riva.

13. Without any intention of making the reader despair or sapping their patience, I transcribe in what follows that which it was possible to recover, mindful of my scanty paleographical resources:

> *Mr Don Bartolo García, For your attention. My dear sir, I greet you with all my plessure. That you can be found in good helth is all that my heart desires. Well I am in good helth. Nothing more than that now I do not egsist at the side of that shameful uncle of mine Julio who why has been the caus of my disgrace where I was condemned to 22 days in prison, there being no need for this with the Q.25 fine, and that's why I left without destination and finding myself in Escuintla I met Pedro Escobar G., and I told him that I did not brung any good address and then he brought me to this farm without electricity and he arranged work for me painting erning 56 cents a day and nowe I have worked for three days and nowe I say that I have more with people from there than not with the family because this work behaved very cruel for me. That's why have said that now I wont grovel because it doesnt soot me because its a lie that my Dad is dead. Not everything is a lie and when I have strength I arriv ther. For nowe still not because I am ashemd for what is happening, and when I go then I tell you my sad storey and I am thinking of you and at your service.*

14. In those days, the judicial summons were small pre-printed papers on the reverse side of which the writ's executing authority wrote the responses to the judge.

15. According to a story born in this era, towards three-thirty in the morning on the day of the execution the police officers mounting guard at Mauricia's door clearly heard the voice of a man inside the cell. (A sweet voice, said one of them, like the litany of the rosary.)

From the Darkness

Possessed of a deep uneasiness, but given the legal prohibitions against opening the door without express authorisation, they immediately raised the alarm about this inexplicable fact. On her arrival, the director of the penal centre showed herself willing to clarify the strange situation. Thus, accompanied by the guards referred to and her own staff, she proceeded without delay to open the door (the only way in). They found no trace of anything. However, hours later, obsessed with leaving no loose ends, the director unofficially ordered an exhaustive investigation of the supposed incident. Its results, as can be presumed, were all negative.

16. According to legend, known and passed on from generation to generation in a low voice and in the penumbra of the night, it was a tree that fed on the blood of those shot.

17. In order to avoid last-minute, unnecessary and inappropriate dramatics, perhaps it would be better at this point to resort to the juridical narration referring to the outcome of the execution:

... the prisoners, having been previously blindfolded, were despatched by force of arms, the individual troops of the first row making the discharge and the Officer under whose command the escort referred to was entrusted with giving the coup de grâce to each of the offenders. Fourth: the Military Surgeon of the Penal Centre Doctor Ángel María Iturbide proceeded to undertake the medico-legal inspection of the bodies of the prisoners, having made the respective declaration of death. Fifth: the previous related aspects now over, the corpses were handed over to Mr Colonel Manuel Maldonado Robles, Director of the Central Penitentiary, to be interred in the respective cemetery according to the legal formalities. The execution ended at six o'clock precisely, having gathered for it the officer in charge, Colonel Miguel Aguilar Peláez, who published the legal proclamation at the first opportunity; Sub-director of the National Police, Colonel Jorge D. Guillén; the Chief of the First Barracks of the Police, Colonel Manuel Arriola Cabrera; and the Chief of the Penal Centre, Colonel Manuel

Oswaldo Salazar

Maldonado Robles; who in keeping with the aforementioned, having read the present document, ratify and sign it with the Undersigned and authorising Secretary.

18. A few hours later, when the edition of *El Imparcial* came out, on its front page was the headline:

ULTIMATE PUNISHMENT CARRIED OUT
Offenders in the Gourd Crime

The essential passages of the news were a brief description of how the events had unfolded: *In the interior of the Central Penitentiary at six o'clock this morning, the offenders who were authors in the Gourd Crime about which we have amply informed our readers, Mauricia Hernández Urbina and Pedro García Gesenäuer, were executed having received the full weight of the law. [Turn to Page 7 Column 5]*

In this sensational trial, all the recourses available in the judicial system of Guatemala, even extending to the resort of seeking a reprieve that is in the power of the President of the Republic, were exhausted. By virtue of having been denied the ultimate recourse, that of a pardon, the offenders received the final notification at six yesterday morning, keeping them in suspense until six o'clock today. The Fifth Court of First Instance, that acted as executor, was ordered to put into effect the so-called 'let it be known and carry out'.

This chapter of the Gourd Crime closes with the application of the death penalty to the second woman ever accused of murder, as well as her accomplice. We know that only very few people gathered at today's execution, among them the Director of La Gaceta de la Policía Nacional, *the learned César Izaguirre, who undertook an interview with the judged woman that will probably be published in the said police organ.*

With this announcement the report in *El Imparcial* ended. Two weeks later, on the 17th of August, ample reportage was published

From the Darkness

on pages 1625-1629 of number 31 of *La Gaceta*. Given its extensive and repetitive content, I transcribe only those extracts that reveal what happened during this interview, as well as the final judgement of the official police narrator:

It is not exactly as the esteemed colleague of El Imparcial *said, that the Director of 'La Gaceta' would have been present at the execution of the prosecuted Hernández Urbina. Yes it is true that the latter was interviewed, but in the prison for women itself, several hours after she had been notified of the terrifying verdict and was now waiting in suspense.*

Hernández Urbina was dressed at the time of our interview, which was at 14.10 on Thursday 31 of July of this year, in a blue-coloured Indian skirt with geometric shapes on little white circles, a dark-coloured apron and a shawl similar in fabric and colour to this. She was cloaked in this last garment, not allowing more than her face and hands to be seen, covered up to the neck. Other than having red eyes, the prisoner did not display major agitation. In the short time in which we saw her, she remained seated at a bench where there was a packet of 'Clowns' cigarettes, a box of matches, a blanket and a small white pillow. On the ground there was a linen sleeping mat; in front of the doorway and inside the room we saw the pale image of Our Lady of the Sorrows in front of which two candles burned and, on the wall a little above the height of the said image, a gold-plated crucifix. In front of the position occupied by the condemned, and hung on the wall, was a picture of the Virgin of Guadalupe.

We sat down before what, when faced by Hernández Urbina, was virtually a corpse, nearly reaching the point of feeling all the respect normally due a human being's mortal remains. We did not want to interrogate her with regard to the crime itself, valuing as more than sufficient the clear and explicit confession that she had volunteered as the trial had unfolded.

Our rapid interrogation developed thus:
"How old are you, madam?"
"I am about 31," she answers with great assurance.

Oswaldo Salazar

"What time did they notify you of the sentence?"

"It would be about eight," she responds, addressing the Director of the penal establishment, who corrects her by indicating that it had been at six in the morning.

"How many years did you and Bartolo García Morán share a household?"

"We were together about 20 years," she responds unhesitatingly.

"Mr Bartolo García Morán was the father of all your children?"

"Yes sir," is the reply.

"Who are the children fathered by him?"

"Rogelia, Manuela and Félix Hernández," she tells us. "Although I had another daughter who was called Tomasa Hernández, fathered by Basilio Peralta before I got together with the deceased."

"Do you believe in God?"

"Why of course, sir!" she affirms without hesitating.

"What religion are you?"

"The Catholic religion," she responds.

"Did you make a confession today?"

"Yes sir."

"Which Father gave you confession?"

"The priest of San Sebastían," she says "but he did not give me absolution."

"Did you confess the whole truth to the priest?"

"Yes sir," she says quickly.

"And do you think he should absolve you?"

"I say, first God," she answers, "but..." (it is announced in the interview that she becomes very worked up from exorcising the extreme thoughts that have enveloped her).

"Are you frightened?"

"I'm scared, very scared..."

"Have you been in captivity before?"

"No sir. Never; nor as a girl..."

"Do you regret everything you have done?"

Under scrutiny and as if obeying a mysterious stroke of conscience, the interrogated woman answers in a very gentle voice:

"Yes sir."

From the Darkness

"Do you believe that it was justice that brought you to this place?"

Avoiding answering the question directly and in a sentence spoken more or less slowly she says:

"What are we to do before the force of destiny!"

As we could see that the interviewee was demonstrating some annoyance with the interview and, feeling just pity for the atrocious situation in which she found herself, we suspended our visit, bidding farewell courteously, which she returned by standing up for an instant.

Two officers of the National Police were guarding the entrance to the enclosure housing the detained woman.

With all the resources that our legal system provides now exhausted, Mauricia Hernández Urbina and Pedro Francisco García Gesenäuer were despatched by force of arms at precisely six o'clock on Friday the first of August of this year. And so was written the epilogue of the fantastic and sensational case, known as the 'Gourd Crime', that so moved public sentiment because of the exaggerated perversity and extreme criminal manner by which it had been committed.

PQ7499.3.S25 P6713 2007x
Salazar, Oswaldo, 1959-
From the darkness